COWBOYS NEVER FOLD

Melissa,
So nice to meet
you!.

Lexi Post

Cowboys Never Fold

LEXI POST

Acknowledgments

To Bob Fabich, my very own cowboy. Thank you for your support and knowledge.

Many people were invaluable resources for this book. Paige Wood who isn't shy about telling me what needs to be fixed and provided a great cover design. I'm so glad you're my sister. Brian Wood who helped me find the right word more times than I can count, including the title. Claire Ashgrove who set me straight on horses and riding naked; lesson well learned. Joanne Mayer for teaching me about poker; the casino lessons were particularly fascinating. Any incorrect information in this story is completely the fault of the author.

I couldn't have produced this book without my critique partner, Marie Patrick and her keen eye and patience. I also want to thank Merritt Crowder for her willingness to read my work and help me make it better.

What wonderful family and friends I have!

AUTHOR'S NOTE

Cowboys Never Fold was inspired by Bret Harte's short story, *The Outcasts of Poker Flat*, first published in 1869. In Harte's story, four members of Poker Flat society—a gambler, a prostitute, a madam, and a drunk—are banned from the western settlement when a sudden urge to be virtuous overtakes the citizens. On their way to the next settlement, the outcasts stop to rest at the base of the high mountains they will need to cross, but as it is November, it is quite cold. An innocent couple, a young man and his fiancée (a tavern waitress), descends from the mountain tops and rests with them. The young man idolizes the poker player and tells him they are going to Poker Flat to marry. The outcasts recognize the goodness of the two young people and adjust their behavior so as not to taint them. As the odd group converse, a blizzard buries them in snow. In the end, none, outcast nor innocent, survive.

But what if the poker player was a woman and the young man a full grown cowboy? Could an outcast and an innocent find a love that could survive both outside forces and their own differences?

Chapter One

Wade Johnson slowed his Chevy Silverado and stared at the wooden sign with burnt-in letters hanging above the dirt road: POKER FLAT NUDIST RESORT.

It swung between two weathered posts, the sign's newness jolting the senses against the Old West background.

Stopping his pickup, he hesitated to make the left turn. His best friend had called in a big favor. Nine years ago, Wade had been blinded by love and almost made the worst mistake of his life. If it hadn't been for Dale's instincts and a paternity test, Wade would have been shackled to a selfish sorority girl and left with another man's kid. Shit, he could have been a country song.

He owed Dale and he'd never back out on a friend, even if it meant working at a nudist resort for three months. "I *am* doing this." The sound of his voice gave him the boost he needed. With his commitment firmly in place despite a dozen misgivings, he turned the truck down the dirt road.

At least the pay was outstanding, and he could choose his own horseflesh and set up the stables as he felt they should be run. Just the thought of starting a new operation had him stepping on the gas a bit harder, his truck throwing up a cloud of dust that could probably be seen in Wickenburg.

After a good mile of nothing but desert, a wooden barrier declared the end of the road. To the right was an overly large garage with only three sides. He brought the truck to a stop underneath the shelter. It could clearly house a couple dozen cars and the massive metal structure was tall enough for RVs too. The roof had to be at least twenty feet high.

Exiting his vehicle, his boots hit concrete. Nice. If this is how the owner built the garage, he couldn't wait to see the new stables. Dale's voice in his head dampened his enthusiasm. *I've sent three men out there to set up this woman's stables and all three quit. This could kill my temp agency's reputation. I need someone I can trust to find out what's going on. If she is a cranky old bitch who expects miracles, I don't need her as a client. But if it's something else, I want to know. If her resort takes off, I plan to be the one filling her staffing needs.*

Wade straightened his black Stetson and walked toward the old man sleeping on a chair in the relative coolness of the structure. It was August and days in the desert usually hit three digit degrees. The sound of his boots hitting the floor didn't wake the man, so he shook him.

"What? What? I don't knows nothin.'" The man's eyes were a bit glazed and his chin showed a few days of beard growth.

Wade tipped his hat. "Afternoon. I'm Wade Johnson. Dale Osborn sent me to set up the stables here."

The man stood and teetered before steadying himself with the folding chair. "I'm Billy." The smell of alcohol was faint but definitely there. Billy thrust out his hand as if suddenly remembering his manners.

Wade shook, taking in the faded blue jeans, ripped sneakers and dirty t-shirt. He sincerely hoped Billy wouldn't be the one greeting the guests. "Where would I find the owner?"

The short man stared at him for a few moments. "Right. Right. Come on. I'll takes you down."

Down? Wade followed Billy to a tan golf cart and got in. As they proceeded out of the garage, he looked everywhere for the supposed resort, but there was nothing but desert for miles, and no butte stood out to hide it.

Then they drove past the wooden barricade and after a few minutes he recognized the edges of what must have been a hundred-year-old ravine that had weathered away to create a small canyon. As they drew closer to the ledge, the resort came into view.

"Wow." It was an ingenious design. One that had him rethinking a few of his own plans for a spread.

Billy smiled a toothy grin. "Yup. That be what everyone says."

Wade shook his head in astonishment. Across the ravine, near the top was a natural shelf of land where a large building, pool and stables sat surrounded by green lawn and narrow pathways for walking. Below that shelf was another that was home to small cottages sporadically placed among the natural desert landscape. There were more walking trails going farther into the small canyon. At the bottom was a creek with a strip of green growth on each side.

"How long did it take to build this place?"

Billy frowned. "If you counts the stonewallin' from the county, two years. But when the permits was in place and legit, the construction took a year. The stables is the newest building." He pointed to the white structure.

Wade's stomach tensed with excitement. A new barn, corral and soon horses of his choosing without spending a dime of his own money was too enticing to pass up, not that he would. Dale's company was new and he needed a good reputation if he was to succeed in Phoenix. Wade owed him and he would stay long enough to discover why the other stablemen left. That Wade would enjoy the job he was hired for was a bonus. He could already see possibilities for trails down to the creek. How far did it go?

"We could has opened sooner if we has reli...help we can depend on. I hope you plan to stay longer than the last horse man." Billy spat over the side of the cart. "We needs someone we can count on out here."

He looked at Billy and his excitement dimmed. "Was the stable manager quitting the only thing that held everything up?"

"Nah. We gots a nosey sheriff and stupid stuff breaks every day." Billy slowed the cart as they drove around a switchback. After the cart rumbled across a well-made wooden bridge that spanned the creek, Billy pointed at the road. "This here path were designed for the wagon and stagecoach. Only the employees gets to drive those. The golf carts, them is for the guests."

"Stagecoach?" Wade scanned the resort as they drove closer, expecting to see the oddity sitting on the verdant lawn.

Billy broke into a big grin, revealing a missing tooth on the left side. "You betcha. Prettiest darn thing I has ever seen. It's a repro...copy of one of them Old West ones. You be in charge of it. Maybe you can give me a ride in it? Miss Kendra don't lets me drive that one."

Wade silently agreed with Miss Kendra's decision. There were a lot of the woman's decisions he agreed with, so why did she have such a hard time keeping staff when she hadn't even opened? It couldn't be because of the nude clientele. She didn't have any yet. He would never have taken a job at a nudist resort if Dale hadn't needed him. People walking around nude in public wasn't his thing.

Oh shit. What if the resort was the owner's retirement dream come true and she ran the place nude? Now that was a sight he wasn't in a hurry to see.

"Here you be. Miss Kendra through that there pavilion. At least, that where I sees her last. She were bossing over the buildin' of some water thingy by the pool. Whatever it are, I sure when she be done, it will look good."

Wade stepped out and tipped his hat. "Thank you." As Billy drove away, Wade shook his head. How could the old man obviously idolize the owner and yet others quit on her? He strolled in the direction Billy indicated. He appreciated the view the resort presented, but he mentally braced himself for encountering a naked old woman.

As he turned the corner at the end of the freestanding pavilion, he found the pool, its crystal-clear water actually making him thirsty. The large rectangle had a curvy pool coming off it that imitated a winding river. Every eight feet or so a concrete high-table broke the surface of the water. Talk about an enticement to drink. Whatever kind of personality this woman had, he would be the first to admit she was smart.

He approached a group of three men with Desert Pool Design emblazoned on their shirts. They rested in the shade, chowing down on sandwiches. "Good afternoon. Could you tell me where to find Miss Kendra Lowe?"

One of the men pointed, his mouth full.

"Thanks."

Wade strode toward the bar. It was under another pavilion, but this one attached to the main building and its far side was supported by stone columns. The sleek wood bar top was at least three inches of ironwood. The rattling of glasses came from behind it but he couldn't see anyone.

"Hello there. I'm looking for Miss Kendra Lowe?"

A young woman stood up from behind the bar, her disheveled dark brown hair caught in a clip behind her head. She wiped sweat from her brow with the back of a dirty hand. It seemed everything was clean but the workers. She gazed at him, no curiosity whatsoever in the deep blue of her eyes. "I'm Kendra Lowe."

Wade couldn't help staring in disbelief. Out of habit, he wiped his hand on his jeans although it was probably cleaner than hers. "Good afternoon, Ms. Lowe. I'm Wade Johnson. Your new stable manager."

She studied him as she shook his hand, her expression revealing nothing.

He, on the other hand, didn't expect the owner of such a pristine spread to be so young, maybe thirty or so, almost his age. Her mouth was wide with a straight nose above it. She had very high cheekbones, but her face held none of the lines of a woman used to manual work, which she appeared to be doing. Her arms were toned, almost muscular as revealed by the modest black tank she wore, though nothing could truly hide the substantial chest it covered. But she was too thin by half, as his grandmother would say.

She placed one dirty hand on her waist and jutted out her hip, giving it a curve that wasn't there before. "So, Cowboy, it appears Dale was successful in finding me another stable manager. Good. I don't have much time left before we open and the trails still need to be chosen, the horses need to be purchased and transported, feed needs to be ordered and a ton of other details I have no clue about. I must have someone who is going to stay at least three months. Can you commit to that, no matter what?"

A surge of adrenaline shot through his body again when she mentioned picking horses. He could pretty much stay however long she needed for a chance to do that. "Yes, Ms. Lowe, I can."

"Good. I can't be worrying about that side of the operation, so you just tell me what you need, Cowboy, and we'll make it happen." She turned toward the main building. "Lacey!"

Wade stared at his new boss. This was a dream job to any cowboy worthy of riding, which made it harder to understand why so many before him quit. Maybe she was really a micromanager and pretended not to be. Or maybe she was too hard to read. Her eyes, a nice royal blue, were anything but windows to her soul. There was no smile of welcome or satisfaction. Even her tone of voice didn't give away anything.

A petite blonde woman came through the glass door of the building and smiled warmly as she approached. "Howdy, I'm Lacey."

Now that was the kind of greeting he liked. He shook her hand, careful not to squeeze too hard.

Kendra leaned on the bar, her substantial chest supported by the dark wood. "Lacey will show you your living quarters. Then become familiar with the stables, corrals and your office. We can meet around nine tonight to discuss next steps."

"Nine, yes Ms. Lowe." He nodded, not sure what to make of the late hour, but she was the boss.

Lacey hooked her arm in his. "Right this way."

"And Cowboy." They'd only taken a couple steps, when Kendra stopped them. "Don't call me Ms. Lowe. It makes me sound like a teacher or something. Kendra will do."

He tipped his hat. "I can do that if you can call me Wade."

Kendra's face didn't even twitch. He waited for a sign from her that she understood. Finally, she nodded once. "Fair enough. See you at nine, Wade."

Kendra watched Wade leave, his tight butt impossible to ignore. Once he was through the glass door into the main building, she let herself slither back over the edge of the bar to sit on the floor. Damn, the man was hot. Why had Dale stopped sending her old codgers? The last thing she needed now was a distraction.

And Wade Johnson was definitely a distraction. His clean-shaven chin could serve as artwork. His brown eyes, which matched his short hair, reminded her of milk chocolate and his voice had her muscles wanting to melt. Thank God she'd been behind the bar because what really had her libido revving was his broad shoulders. Only a muscular man could be that thin at the waist and have such broad shoulders. Dammit. She hadn't had sex since she bought Poker Flat and she'd be damned if she'd have it now with some hunky cowboy employee. The odds were stacked against that working out well.

Refocusing, she pulled the small cooler back into place, assuring it would drain through the floor and not all over it. At least she wouldn't have to worry about the cowboy being underfoot. He had his domain and she had hers. She just needed to make it through their meeting tonight. After wiping her hands on her work jeans, she picked up the glass washer and set it in the sink. The plumber would be in tomorrow morning to take care of installing the final pieces of the bar according to code. Luckily, she had the liquor license from the last owner of the Poker Flat Bar, which had been located where her garage now stood. That license was worth every penny she'd paid for the ramshackle building she tore down.

And having Adriana as the bartender of her new bar should keep the liquor sales high, *if* the woman kept her clothes on. Kendra wiped her hands on a bar towel and shook her head. She had quite the crew here, but she knew all of them and their weaknesses. All she had to do is discover Wade Johnson's weakness and she could feel comfortable because right now he seemed too perfect and that would never work here. She threw the towel over the towel rack and stepped out from behind the bar.

Thankfully, she'd instituted the rule that all employees must be clothed while on shift. She'd found that tidbit in her research on nudist resorts. There was no way she'd be able to keep her hands off her new cowboy if he decided to get naked. And there was no way Adriana would be able to keep her legs closed with that man around. A former prostitute, Adriana still loved sex, but she also loved not having to do it for the money.

As if she'd known she was being thought of, Adriana pushed open the glass door to the outdoor/indoor bar. She held a tray of glasses filled with what appeared to be iced tea. Her skimpy jean shorts and red-checkered halter had her looking like a Mexican Daisy Duke. Kendra admired the woman on that level. Her comfort with her sexuality was impressive. As a teenager, Kendra's own substantial chest had simply added to her aura of trailer trash so she kept it well covered most of the time.

"Hey, boss, I thought the pool workers would like a refreshing cold drink." Adriana raised her hand. "All non-alcoholic, of course."

"Fine, but then they need to get back to work. They've been eating their lunches for an hour. I'm not paying them to take a siesta."

"You got it." Adriana's smile was wide as she tossed her straight black hair over her shoulder and sauntered out beyond the pavilion.

Kendra shook her head and sighed before heading inside. She could tell Adriana was much happier than she'd been when Kendra met her in Storey County, Nevada, during a small poker tournament. She hadn't planned on playing that one, but at the last minute had skipped Reno to avoid a possible awkward meeting with her ex-husband. When she decided to open a nudist resort, Adriana had come to mind immediately as someone who wouldn't care about a bunch of naked people running around.

Striding through the large gathering room with its twelve-foot-wide stone fireplace, Kendra allowed herself a secret smile. The contractor had thought the fireplace would be too big, but even he acknowledged how awesome it looked in the great room. It had become the centerpiece of the main building.

Walking through one of the cozy dining rooms, she pushed open the batwing doors to the kitchen. The spotless, stainless steel area was the domain of her cook, Selma, who was, as usual, muttering to herself in Spanish.

Kendra opened the refrigerator and grabbed a protein shake. She hadn't had lunch, but she didn't have time to stop for it either. Walking over to the shiny dishwasher, she listened to the hum as it sanitized its contents then crouched and looked beneath it to be sure everything was draining properly. Two nights ago, that had not been the case. If it was having issues, she would add it to her list for the plumber tomorrow. All appeared fine, so that meant one less task for the man.

She stood, then walked to where Selma cut vegetables on the stainless steel counter. She went at the food like a lumberjack at a tree, but Kendra couldn't fault the results. "Selma, any other plumbing problems I need to have the plumber take a look at tomorrow?"

The older woman didn't stop slicing. "Yeah, the hand sink is clogged. There's no fucking reason why it should be that way. I only wash my hands there. I take as good care of my kitchen here as I did of my girls in Carlin. I'm telling you, either there is a curse upon this place, or someone is messing with us."

Selma's brothel had been the best on Interstate 80 until, according to the ex-madam, a curse had been laid upon it. So it was no surprise this was her latest theory regarding the many hiccups they'd encountered in getting the resort ready, but Kendra honestly believed it was simply how things went these days. Faulty products, ignorant installers, cracks due to shipping, etcetera, had easily explained the hurdles she'd had to jump over. "Okay, I'll have him look at it tomorrow. Hopefully, that will be the end of it."

Selma grumbled something unintelligible that Kendra had a feeling wasn't meant for her ears, so she grabbed up her shake and took a swallow as she exited the kitchen. Striding toward the front desk, she noticed Wade and Lacey getting into a golf cart. Now why did Lacey have to show him where the stables were? Couldn't he see them for himself?

Irritation had her taking another swallow. Pushing open one of the tall tinted doors that welcomed visitors to the resort, she stepped out into the heat.

Lacey was explaining. "Don't worry, it's actually a rule that we keep our clothes on during our shift. Just be forewarned, Adriana does like men, so you may want to be on your guard with her."

Wade smiled. "Good to know."

Kendra gritted her teeth. The cowboy didn't need a personal escort to the stables. Her bookkeeper/receptionist had a lot of work to do. "Lacey, did you show Wade his casita?"

The pretty girl started as if she'd been caught doing something she shouldn't. "Oh, I didn't know you were here. Yes, I did. I was going to explain the stables to Wade, but I need to reconcile the bedding shipment with what we received."

Kendra's muscles relaxed. "Go ahead and do the shipment. I'll point out the way. We're shorthanded as it is and your abilities are critical to Poker Flat."

Lacey blushed. "Okay. Thanks."

As Lacey walked into the building, Kendra studied the cowboy. He considered her with equal interest, but it wasn't admiration. He appeared puzzled and that gave her a certain amount of satisfaction. She never revealed her hand.

Strolling over to the cart, she took one more swallow of her shake. "Have you ever driven a golf cart?"

The brim of his hat shaded his face, but his expression was easily read. "Yes, actually. I helped my little sister with a few of her golf tournament fundraisers."

Oh boy, this cowboy was far too good for the likes of Poker Flat. One more reason for her to stay away. "Good. Then take the path marked with the horse's head. We made all the signs easy for guests to follow."

He looked at the sign, putting his face in profile again. Shit, he was as handsome from the side as from the front. She had the unusual urge to nip at his jawline.

"That's smart. I wish all vacation spots did that."

His compliment surprised her, and she shifted her weight to her right leg, jutting out her hip. "I had to do that because our employee base isn't large and I didn't want to waste staff positions on golf cart drivers."

He turned back to her and smiled. "Another smart idea."

Completely uncomfortable with his praise and inviting smile, she ignored his comment. "In your office you should find enough to get started. Make a list of anything there you need as well as anything else for marking trails and suggestions for horses. I plan on having guests chauffeured from the garage to the resort in a wagon and I want to offer trail rides for those who are more adventurous. Remember, all guests will be nude, so if there are any special supplies we need in order to make sitting a horse comfortable, write them down too."

His smile disappeared. "Wait, you want people to ride horses while naked?"

"Of course. This is a nudist resort."

"I'm sorry, but you can't do that."

She opened her mouth to tell him she could do whatever she wanted, but he kept talking.

"If a person rides naked, they will have burns not only on their legs where they brush the saddle, but also in other areas that I guarantee you they will not be happy about."

She pondered that for a moment. Maybe that was why no other resort offered nude horseback riding, why Buddy and Ginger had longed for that experience so much. So if she could figure it out, it would make her place even more unique than it was. "I'm sure we can come up with a way around that. We'll go over it tonight."

He frowned and her stomach tensed. "Dinner is at six. Don't be late. You don't want to miss Selma's cooking and you don't want to make her mad at you either."

"Why Ms. Lowe?"

"Trust me. I was late one night and I found my quesadilla riddled with hot pepper sauce so fiery it burned my mouth for two days. You're better off not showing up at all."

He grinned and her stomach relaxed. "Okay, I'll be on time."

"Good, and Wade…"

"Yes."

"I'm not high society and I'm not married anymore, so as I said before, we can drop the Ms. Lowe."

He bowed his head and she could have sworn he was hiding a smile, but when he looked at her, he was dead serious. "I'll remember that, Kendra."

Her throat closed as he spoke her name, a strong rush of heat invading her body. Nodding once, she turned around and strode back to the building, throwing her empty shake can in the trash outside before stepping into the coolness of the resort.

Damn, she liked the sound of her name on his lips. Staying away from that cowboy was going to be very, very hard.

CHAPTER TWO

Wade admired the swing of his new boss's hips and smirked. The blasted woman hadn't smiled yet, but he would make her. Not delving into why that was important to him, he climbed into the golf cart. Turning the quiet vehicle on, he slowly maneuvered it around the fountain that welcomed guests and followed the path to the stables.

When he arrived and stepped out, he couldn't help letting out a low whistle. The stables were perfect. He'd seen new stables before, but these had been well planned and the materials were quality. His estimation of Kendra Lowe rose another notch. Whether it was her or her ability to allow her stable manager to do his work didn't matter.

The building was painted white, which would gray with age, and there was an outside wash area that included a shower for workers. Inside were six stalls on each side along with an area for tack and an area for feed. Across from that was the wagon Kendra mentioned. Billy was right, it was a sweet reproduction that looked authentic, but with extra shocks to cushion the ride for modern passengers and their luggage. He didn't see a stagecoach in this building. Maybe it was for show, like the waterfall by the pool, and was somewhere else on the property.

Wade strolled through the barn, his anticipation building as he envisioned horses, hay and saddles in all their assigned places. When he stepped out the back, he found a corral and farther off was additional fencing to allow the horses to graze and run. Next to the barn was another, smaller building with a large metal one attached out back.

Returning through the stables, he entered the smaller building to find it housed his office along with a bathroom, break room and a waiting area for guests. At the end of the hall, he opened another door and halted. "Holy shit."

In the middle of a steel garage structure stood a red-lacquered stagecoach. Stepping closer, he could see it was also a reproduction, but it was stellar. He ran his hand along the frame and finally opened the door. "This had to have cost a fortune." As he hiked himself up, the coach rocked sideways. He sat on one of the leather seats and peered through the open window to view the suspension. Large leather straps held the seating compartment above the axles. If the stagecoach had been outside, he would have thought he'd stepped back in time, but it wasn't. His view was the metal walls of the building. After jumping down, he closed the door carefully. Without a second thought, he pulled himself up to the driver's seat.

Maybe it was the kid in him, but the adrenaline rush of being atop such a fascinating vehicle had him itching to drive it.

He chuckled as he looked about him. There were no reins to flick without horses, but there was an emergency brake and he worked it a couple times.

Where the hell did this woman's money come from? Was that what had his predecessors leaving? Did they discover she had stolen the money or worse, was connected to a drug ring or something? He just couldn't see her as having been born rich. Rich people did not get their hands dirty like this woman did. Had his predecessors discovered she had links to a drug cartel? Out here in the desert would be a perfect hiding spot. If Dale was linked to something like that, his fledging business would die a quick death. Concern tightened Wade's stomach. He needed to stay focused on his investigation. That was his priority.

He certainly wasn't going to find out anything sitting on top of a stagecoach to nowhere. He climbed down and headed for the exit. He had an obligation to fulfill to Dale and also to Kendra and playing around wasn't going to get it done. Closing the door to the garage without a backward glance, Wade stepped into his office and set his hat on the file cabinet.

Settling into the comfortable leather chair, he flicked on the computer. More than a dozen folders popped up all clearly labeled, but there were dozens of files outside those folders. Opening one titled "Horses," he perused the contents. There was good research already done there. Closing the folder, he scanned the others. One was titled "Misc." Curious, he opened it. Scanned copies of receipts for what looked like trips were the first twenty. Clicking on another, he found a list of all the employees. Hmm, maybe the last stable manager wasn't good with names as there was a description next to each.

He frowned at the phrase next to Kendra's name—"big boobs." That wasn't right. Reading more carefully, he found a lot of derogatory comments next to the female employees. Next to Adriana's name it read "good lay." He quickly deleted the file. Didn't the man realize Kendra could look at his computer files at any time?

Disturbed, Wade scanned the rest of the file titles until he came across a bunch that started with an X. Curious, he opened one. "Fucking asshole." The file was a photo of a woman's pussy, her legs spread wide, her fingers playing with her clit. He clicked on properties and was somewhat relieved the image was from an internet site and not taken by the former employee. To make sure, he pulled up another random X file and found another pornographic image. Again it focused on a woman's pussy, but this one had a dark cock just starting penetration. The woman's blue fingernails were the same as in the other photo. This picture also had a view of the woman's breasts as well, her hardened nubs sporting dangling nipple clips. Wade quickly closed the file. Darkening all the X files, he dumped them in the trash and emptied it.

Despite his disgust that his predecessor had stored pornography on his work computer, Wade wasn't immune to the visual stimulation, and the tightening in his jeans bothered him. He looked in the drawers of the desk and pulled out a pen and paper. Grabbing his hat, he headed for the stables. An inventory of what would be needed should cure his sudden hard-on.

He'd barely stepped into the relative cool of the barn when the buzz of a golf cart caught his attention as it crunched over the desert gravel in front of his office. Stepping outside, he found Billy sitting at the wheel and a man in uniform getting out. "Can I help you?"

The man halted and turned his footsteps toward him. As he drew closer, Wade recognized the sheriff uniform. The man stopped in front of him and held out his hand. "Good afternoon, I'm Deputy Sheriff Harper."

Wade gave the sheriff's hand a good shake, not missing how the man sized him up. "Is there a problem?"

Sheriff Harper touched the brim of his hat. "No, not at all. I come out here often to make sure all is okay. This is such an isolated spot and with Kendra being a lone woman, I like to be sure no one is hassling her."

Instinct had Wade covering his reactions. No sheriff did that unless there were ulterior motives. "I haven't met him yet, but I understand she does have a security guard. Is there reason for concern? Do you think she should hire more security?"

"My main concern is that this is a nudist resort and who knows what kind of crazies will be coming here. I've tried to get her to hire more guards, but she won't hear of it. So I make sure I come out here often." Harper tugged on his gun belt, a move not lost on Wade. "So when did you start working here? Last I knew Michael had quit."

"Just started today. Have to say, these facilities are excellent." He grinned widely. He could play the single-minded cowboy with the best of them. "Can't wait to fill this barn with horses."

"Horses. Right."

Harper stared openly at him and he kept his wide smile in place. Let the man think he was too interested in horses to notice anything else, but Wade's instinct told him to keep an eye on Harper.

"Well, I'd best get going." The sheriff grinned. "I want to stop in and see how Kendra is. I know she appreciates having a man she can call on."

Wade nodded and headed back into the barn. He felt the sheriff's eyes on him, so he stopped in front of the wagon since it was near the entrance and wrote on his pad of paper, *matching quarter horses. What's up with Harper? Interested in Kendra? Not going to happen. Clueless.* He turned to keep the man in his sight.

Billy honked the pathetic horn on the golf cart and Wade gave what he hoped was a disinterested wave, but the sheriff definitely had his interest.

~~~~~~

Kendra looked up from her computer at the knock on her office door. "Enter if you dare."

The cowboy stepped in. "You did say nine."

Her body revved at the sight of him and she glanced at the clock instead. "It's nine already?"

Wade strode forward and took the leather wingback chair in front of her desk. His shoulders spanned it as if it were made for him. The chair swallowed everyone else, not that she should be thinking about his shoulders right now.

"You missed dinner."

"Yes. That happens a lot. We are very close to opening and there are a thousand details to attend to. One of the perks of being the owner." She shrugged.

"You lost out on some amazing enchiladas. Selma gave me a couple extra for a midnight snack." He grinned.

"Selma gave you extras?" Selma never gave anyone to-go plates.

"Yup. And when I told her how much I loved cornbread, she promised to make it on Friday with her chili. You have hired a fantastic cook."

"I know." Selma was crankier than a javelina. What made the cowboy so special, besides his broad shoulders, chiseled face and laze-the-day-away eyes?

He leaned forward, the scent of men's soap, just a slight whiff, filled her nostrils. "I didn't get her in trouble, did I?"

Clean and fresh like a perfect summer day spent at a picnic in the grass. Kendra shook her head, mainly to dispel the pleasurable feeling he conjured up for her. "No, of course not. I want my employees to get along. If she gave you extra food because she likes you, that's a good thing." She minimized the screen she'd been working on and stood.

His gaze swept over her and she was suddenly conscious of being in the same sweaty clothes she'd been in since this afternoon. She certainly wasn't going to apologize to an employee, although something made her want to. "Did you make that list I asked for?"

"Yes, Ms.—Kendra." He reached into his back pocket and pulled out folded papers.

"Good. Let's go over to my table where the lighting is better." She waited for him to step to the right, but instead he backed up and waited for her to pass. No one treated her like that and it took her a moment to move forward.

Walking past him, she pretended she was used to being thought of as a lady and sat on the far side of the table to keep some distance. But damn if the man didn't take the chair next to her, filling her nostrils with his clean scent and presenting her with his stunning profile as he spread the papers out on the table.

"The basic layout of the barn is good. I've separated these sheets by project. This one has suggestions for horses. This one is the supplies for the horses. This one is the supplies for trail riding, and this one is for the wagon."

Kendra couldn't help staring at his mouth as he spoke. His enthusiasm brought quick smiles between his sentences. He was excited about the stable. That was good, good for the resort. "This is almost as organized as Lacey. We have two weeks. Can you do all this in that timeframe? Because if you can't, I would suggest prioritizing the wagon and those horses and feed and such."

He pointed to the paper closest to her and she admired his dark forearm. He must wear his sleeves rolled up to the elbows often because the hair on his arm was almost invisible against the tanned skin.

"I did that, but I think we can be ready. On the back of this I have sketched out some possible trails."

She tried to study the paper, but she was fascinated by his large hands. How did they hold something as small as a pen? She was used to men who played poker, many of whom had smaller hands than Wade's, some were even manicured. This cowboy had man's hands.

"Kendra? What do you think?"

She turned to look at him and found his face no more than six inches from hers. She could control her facial features, but she had no dominion over her racing heart. "I think you should move forward as you have planned here."

His weight shifted toward her, just a slight movement, one most people wouldn't notice, but her past profession had her picking up on everything.

"Good. If you give me free rein, I promise you, you'll be happy."

Her breath caught at the idea of giving him the freedom of her body. To feel his rough, large hands brush across her nipples would be exquisite. "I'm going to hold you to that promise, Cow—Wade."

His lips twitched into a seductive smirk. "I always keep my promises."

Heat infused her body and suddenly even her tank top felt too warm, too confining. Is that how the nudists felt all the time? If so, she had a new sympathy for them.

The gentle touch of his hand on her cheek jolted her from her stupor.

"Hey, are you okay? You look overheated."

In her rush to get away, she stood and his hand brushed the side of her breast, sending the heat spiraling down between her legs. She stumbled against her chair and it tipped backward. She caught it just as he reached for it.

Their bodies collided. He grasped her arms, which kept her from falling. "Whoa, where are you going?"

That was a good question. The heat of his body against hers made everything worse—or better—depending on how she wanted to look at it. She braced her hands against his chest. "I think I've just been cooped up in this office too long. I need to stretch my legs."

He slid his arm around her back, turning her toward the door. "I think what you need is food."

She wanted to argue, but the pressure of his arm against her spine had her obeying as he led her out to the main room, his touch never leaving her, despite the fact he opened every door with his other hand.

Once they were in the kitchen, he made her sit on a stool. He rubbed her shoulders with his strong hands as he faced her. "Now you aren't going to faint on me while I make you something to eat, are you?"

She shook her head, too rattled to argue. She was his boss. He was her employee, although a temporary one. All the more reason she should keep her hands to herself. It wasn't as if she hadn't seen a good-looking man before. It must be her lack of sexual activity over the past couple years. She poured every ounce of energy she had into Poker Flat. She needed to keep her dream in front of her. This venture was for Buddy and Ginger wherever they were. No one could judge them for being nudists or her for her roots anymore. No one could claim her not worthy enough or take Poker Flat away. This time she called the game.

Wade moved about the kitchen with confidence, causing her admiration to grow. Now if he would just take off that blue-and-white-checkered shirt so she could see the hard chest she felt beneath her hands in her office, she would be completely happy... for the moment.

Poker Flat. Concentrate.

Wade sliced tomatoes as if he were born doing it, and she closed her eyes. She tried to remember the profit-and-loss statement Lacey gave her that very afternoon, her to-do list, his to-do list, his hands as he pointed to the different pages. Ugh. She opened her eyes in time to see him lathering a piece of rye bread with mayonnaise, his hand gently cradling the bread.

Poker Flat. Focus, Kendra, focus.

Topping the sandwich, he sliced through it twice, making four triangles. He picked up the plate and walked around the stainless steel table he'd been working on. He stopped in front of her and, lifting one of the triangles, he raised it even with her mouth. "Okay, time to eat."

She cocked her head as she lost herself for a moment in his dark eyes. "I'm a big girl, Wade. I can feed myself."

"That may be true, but I have little faith you will. Something else will come up and you will forget this masterpiece of a sandwich I made." The self-deprecating grin he gave her pulled at her heartstrings.

"Fine." She opened her mouth and he gently inserted the point of the sandwich. She bit down and pulled back quickly, but the flavors of turkey, tomato, mayo, provolone and a hint of horseradish had her mouth celebrating. "Wow, you *are* a food artist."

"Trying to butter me up won't work. Here." Willingly, she opened her mouth again, and he inserted the sandwich. Grasping his wrist, she took the rest of the piece from him.

The flavors were perfect together. Who knew? "Where did you learn to make sandwiches like that?"

He shrugged. "I didn't. It took me a long time to master the art of budgeting while in college. Too often I had very little food in the fridge and was too proud to drop by my mom and dad's for dinner, so I got creative with the few ingredients I did have." He picked up another triangle.

She opened her mouth and bit the piece in half.

"Trust me. Not all my creations came out this good."

She swallowed quickly, her curiosity piqued. "What was your worst?"

He held up the other half of the triangle, and she carefully took it from him with her teeth before maneuvering it into her mouth.

"I'd have to say the night I added ketchup to my Captain Crunch cereal. I had no milk, no meat and wasn't getting paid for two more days."

He grimaced and a vision of what he must have looked like back then flashed through her mind. "I'm pretty sure I wouldn't have liked that either. Have you ever tried making the box macaroni and cheese with—"

Wade inserted another quarter of the sandwich into her mouth and she squinted her eyes at him while she chewed.

"No talking until you finish this entire sandwich."

"Excuse me, but I'm the—" Wade filled her mouth with sandwich and she bit down lightly on his fingers.

"Hey." He pulled his hand away and examined it for bite marks. "I don't remember Dale saying anything about this being a dangerous job."

"That's what you get when you force feed your boss."

He studied her a moment, probably trying to figure out if she was joking.

She wasn't. She was in charge and no matter how handsome he was, he wasn't going to control her. "So are you going to let me have the last piece or not?"

He handed her the plate. "Of course."

His body language told her she acted like a bitch. Yeah, maybe she did. She wanted to redirect his attention, but couldn't think of anything, so she stuffed the last quarter of the sandwich in her mouth and chewed.

He took the plate from her and brought it to the sink. "I'll just wash these up for Selma and head to bed."

She was off the stool and grabbing the sprayer before he could reach it. "No. You made the meal for me. I can clean up. You've probably had a long day. When did you get up?"

He shrugged. "Probably around five. I didn't really pay attention."

"Exactly. I'll stay and clean up. Go get a good night's sleep. You have a lot of ordering to do tomorrow based on your lists."

His eyes widened. "You really approve of everything?"

She put her other hand on her hip. "Listen. I don't know anything about horses. All I know is what nudists like based on research. I'll come up with something for the nude riding, but I need an expert to set up my stables and trails. You're that expert. I'm not going to get in the way of that."

He smiled, his eyes almost twinkling in his excitement. "Well then, boss. I definitely need to be doing the dishes for you."

He reached for the sprayer and without thinking, she pulled it out and sprayed him.

CHAPTER THREE

"Oh my God, I'm sorry. I didn't mean to." She stared as the shirt conformed to Wade's body, the contours of his chest coming out in full relief. Turning away from the titillating sight, she grabbed a couple hand towels hanging next to the sink. She just didn't want him to do the dishes. Now he would think she was the worst boss in the state.

Turning back to help him dry off, she froze. Wade had taken off his shirt, revealing his moist chest and arms. The man's pectorals were what she called mountain muscles and the wet hair that formed a line straight down the middle of his rippled abdominals disappeared beneath blue jeans being held up by a big-buckled belt. She tried to look at his face but was drawn to his large biceps, which had been hidden by the shirt. She followed those to his shoulders where more muscle explained why he appeared so broad. He was. The man was walking muscle.

"Are those for me?"

His voice snapped her out of her drool-like state, and she looked him in the eye. The man's lips formed a slow smirk.

"Yes. Here." She gave him the towels and he pushed one back at her.

"Can you dry my back? That water sprayer is strong."

"Right, of course." She was bumbling like an idiot, but what woman wouldn't be. Damn, the man was built. He made her feel petite despite being taller than average. He had to be well over six feet. Stepping behind him, she was treated to another tantalizing view. As he wiped at his chest and arms, the muscles in his back danced, showing the many layers he had. She hesitated to touch him. He would be warm and so male.

"Isn't it wet?" He rolled his shoulders. "It feels like it."

"Yes. Yes, it is." She forced herself to use the towel against his skin, careful not to let her hand touch him. If it did, she wouldn't be able to stop. She wiped at the moisture until he was dry, then took a deep breath and stepped around him, tossing the towel on the sink. "I'm sorry. I was just trying to keep you from washing the dishes."

"No harm. I've been wet before." His smile appeared again, and she had the strongest urge to kiss it.

Switching her weight to her right hip, she crossed her arms. "Well, I guess now you have to let me do the dishes." She meant to sound flippant, but didn't carry it off well.

He held out his towel. "Yup. Definitely got your way...this time."

She uncrossed her arms to take the towel and crushed it against her chest. "Have a good night."

He shrugged his large shoulders, causing her insides to tighten. Why did she have to be so susceptible to broad shoulders, and why did he have to have the most muscular ones she'd ever seen?

"It all depends on the bed." He winked and brushed past her. Their arms touched for a second, his clean male scent, which was stronger now without his shirt, washed over her and almost buckled her knees.

She couldn't resist and turned to watch him walk away, his back teasing her with its muscle play until the batwing doors swung closed behind him.

She pulled the damp towel up to her face and inhaled. God, the man smelled good. Damn. Built, well mannered, organized, knowledgeable and with a dark tan above his waist that made her want to crawl down his pants to see how far it went.

She groaned. Tan to the waist meant he was outside without a shirt more often than not. "Hell." She was definitely screwed…or rather wanted to be. Could she ask Dale for another replacement stable manager?

Wade strode through the open dining area and outside, hoping for some cooler air, but it was almost as hot as his skin where his arm had brushed by his boss's on the way out. The desert summer nights had yet to give way to the cooler fall temperatures and added to his already over-sensitized body.

Ignoring the golf cart he'd been assigned by Lacey, he took the opportunity to walk to his casita. The dark sky shimmered with millions of stars and he attempted to focus on it instead of the desire he'd seen in Kendra's eyes. When she turned around with the towels it was as if he'd been gut-punched. Her stare had devoured him in a very flattering way. He'd never seen such honest interest from a woman before. She didn't even seem aware she'd been doing it, probably because she didn't show any emotion normally.

As she wiped down his back, she's stroked him sensuously, causing his cock to harden in his jeans. He had to get out of there. By time she stood in front of him with arms folded beneath her impressive bustline, he'd become very uncomfortable.

He stumbled over a rock and brought his gaze back to the dark path. Falling in bed with the boss was not an option. He had to keep his two priorities in mind. Do the job he was hired to do because he would be paid very well to do it and find out why the other men quit. Dale had made it clear Wade was the only man he trusted to discover what was wrong with Poker Flat.

He came to a stop, his heated body cooling. Was that why the other men quit? She wanted them in bed or they wanted into her bed and she said no? Is that what the last guy had been hoping for? The thought had him clenching his fists. He'd run in to men like that. Men who could tame a wild horse but didn't have a clue how to treat a lady. Or maybe they couldn't stand taking orders from a lady.

Forcing himself to unclench his hands, he continued to his lodging. Kendra seemed well able to handle herself and her staff. Even better, it appeared some of them were incredibly loyal. He'd get to know each of them more, find out why they liked her or didn't. Someone was the key to why the other cowboys quit and it could very well be Kendra.

After unlocking the door to his new home, he stepped into the cool interior. The air conditioner hummed smoothly as it should, being brand new. He found the thermostat and turned it off. He much preferred the sounds of the desert. His casita was at the end of the row of staff cottages, so he opened windows on three sides, leaving the one toward the place next door closed.

He looked at his duffle bag of clothes and his equipment thrown on the couch, but didn't move to unpack. It was late and he was more than ready for sleep. Dropping his hat on the dresser, he sat on the bed and pulled off his boots. In no time his jeans and underwear followed and he lay down, his hands behind his head.

Kendra was a puzzle. She was obviously very smart but stoic. The first real emotion he'd seen in her had been tonight. Just the thought of her eyes at that moment caused his balls to tighten. He'd tried not to think of her in that way, but the minute she'd stared at him with so much desire, he'd become aware of her as a woman first and his boss second.

Every feminine aspect of her flooded his senses from her stunning blue eyes to her full red lips. He'd like to see her with her hair down, but he doubted that would happen while the resort was in preparation to open. The woman worked hard. Something drove her.

Would she be like that in bed? Would she take charge or give up her control? His cock jerked at the thought. There was nothing like having a strong woman under him to rev his senses. The challenge and the equal passion had always been what he'd looked for in a lover. He would like to have her ride him first. Let her feel in control as she sheathed him inside her wet pussy. He would lift his hips high, giving her all he had as she rocked against him, her clit brushing against the hair above his dick, her large breasts swaying above him. He couldn't resist. He would take one of her hard nipples into his mouth even as she ground against him. Sucking and nibbling, even holding tight with his teeth if she tried to break free.

Wade closed his eyes as his hand gripped his cock. Shit, what had he'd been thinking? He couldn't fantasize about a woman he was supposed to be secretly investigating, about setting her on the stainless steel table in the kitchen and pulling her black tank below her breasts. Unhooking her bra so her nipples could be free for him to suck on as his fingers played inside her jeans, circling her clit until she rocked into his hand. He wouldn't bring her release though. He'd pull her jeans off and lay her back on the cool metal. Then he'd spread her legs wide and push his cock into her moist sheath. He'd hold her hips as he pulled out and pushed back in, her pussy tightening around him, resisting his exit. He'd increase his rhythm, pumping into her, hearing her whimper with pleasure until he reached between them and rubbed her juices over her excited nub. He could hear her scream as she reached her orgasm, and he stiffened as he filled her with all he had.

The howl of a coyote brought him back to his room and his wet hand. "Fuck."

~~~~~

Kendra joggled and poked at the flue handle with the butt of her screwdriver. The thing barely budged. "Come on, you freakin' pile of rocks. Give it up already." Crawling out of the fireplace, she jiggled the handle then crawled back in for the third time and hit the damper hard. Nothing happened, not even a crack of light shone through it. "To hell with you then." She slammed her elbow up against the metal, but pulled it back into her body fast. "Ow! Damn waste of space." She slammed the butt of the screwdriver against it for good measure and received a face full of garbage.

Spitting out the dust and dirt, she stared at the pile on the hearth. "I don't believe it." Sticks and feathers covered the area along with pieces of paper cups and a candy wrapper. Peeking up the now open flu, she could see more garbage and bird nest remnants.

"It could be worse." The male voice behind her had her taking a deep breath only to cough at the dust in her lungs. She crawled out and turned to Sheriff Harper. "How could it be worse?"

He grinned. "It could have been bats."

It took all her willpower not to roll her eyes. "How can I help you, Sheriff?"

The man shook his head. "I don't think I'm the one who needs help around here, and I told you, call me Clive."

She turned her back on the man and lifted her gray t-shirt to wipe off her face. Then she bent over and picked up her tools. She didn't need eyes in back of her head to know he stared at her ass. He was a nice guy, but he needed to move on. She wasn't interested nor was she as helpless as he wanted her to be. She turned to face him. "No, actually I'm good now."

He stroked his chin. "You're going to need someone to clean out that chimney. Don't want your first fire in that thing to burn this whole building down."

"Yeah, I know." She strode toward her office, the sheriff following her. "That's why I opened the flue. I have someone coming tomorrow."

"You certainly seem to have everything covered." He sounded irritated.

She glanced back at him as she set the toolbox on her desk. The man had to stop coming by the resort every couple days. She'd like to think he really looked out for the place, but she'd put money down he either wanted to have sex with her or hoped to gawk at some of her naked guests. She turned, heading back out, forcing him to move aside as she closed her door, careful to lock it behind her.

He walked with her. "How much longer before you open?"

She shrugged, well aware she had reservations for eight people the week after next. "Maybe in a couple weeks, if I don't have any more problems."

Harper took off his hat and ran his hand through his hair, a favorite pastime of his. She wasn't sure why since he kept it military style, barely an inch of his dark buzz was visible. He placed his hat back on. "You have definitely been having your share of problems. Doesn't that worry you?"

No, what worried her was his constant presence at the resort. She needed to get rid of him and she had an idea of how to do it. "Not really. All new places have to work out the kinks, even after they open." Like that new casino in Vegas she stayed at three years ago. She was one of their first guests and treated to cold showers for two days of playing thanks to a faulty part in the hot water heater.

She exited the building and headed for the cart. The sheriff was like a gnat that wouldn't go away.

"What if—"

"Sheriff, if you want to talk you'll have to come with me." She got in the golf cart and as she suspected, he joined her. Stepping on the accelerator, she headed for the stables.

The sheriff didn't miss a beat. "What if your place over on this side of the canyon was built on an old burial ground or something? That could mean problems forever."

She had to hand it to the man, he was tenacious. "Nope, no chance of that. Not only did I research the history of this land, but I also went to the Tribal Council to find out the real story. No burial ground anywhere within fifteen miles of this place."

"Hmm, that's quite specific."

Yeah, it was also a complete bluff. She had no clue where the closest burial ground was, but he didn't need to know that. Rounding a bend in the path, the cart made a slow ascent toward the stables. She'd avoided this part of the resort for three days now. She'd also avoided being anywhere near Wade Johnson that entire time.

But she had business to attend to with him and having the sheriff along might help keep her sex drive in check and make it clear to the sheriff she didn't need him. Killing two birds with one stone as the old proverb said, worked for her.

As she pulled to a stop, she didn't see her stable manager anywhere. She exited the cart and stood for a moment, ignoring Harper. Wade was either in his office or the barn. Since the barn was closer, she headed there. She turned the corner of the stables and halted. The sheriff bumped into her and politely apologized, but she couldn't have cared less.

Standing in the middle of the tack area with his shirt off was Wade. He was brushing down a gorgeous light-colored horse. The movement of his arms was sensual as he stroked the tall beast. His back had a sheen on it from sweat.

Harper interrupted her thoughts. "That's a beauty. Where did you get him?"

She wanted to say from a temp agency, but caught herself just in time. "You'll have to ask Wade."

At the sound of her voice, he turned around, and she swallowed a groan. His chest was as sweaty as his back and he looked as if she'd just doused him with water. All the salacious feelings she had for him three nights ago in the kitchen flooded back and her body flushed.

Harper's voice interrupted her enjoyable view of Wade. "You don't know where he got this horse? How can you let an employee take on that kind of responsibility? How do you know he won't overcharge you? Did you do a background check on him?"

Wade scowled and she didn't blame him. What right did this man, sheriff or not, have to question how she ran her business? "As a matter of fact I did, and he is squeaky clean. In fact, one of his references was from a Superior Court judge. You can't beat that." She stepped away from Harper and winked at Wade.

He grinned at the sheriff. "Yup." Then he looked at her full on and every nerve ending prickled with sexual awareness. "I started with a matching pair of blonde Belgians. This is Sage and that's Daisy. They'll pull your wagon for the arriving guests."

She took the opportunity to tear her gaze away from his and look at the opposite stall. Taking a deep breath, she moved closer to view Daisy. She had to admit she was impressed with the beauty and size of the horses and she had a feeling her guests would be as well. "They're gorgeous."

Harper came up from behind her, stepping far too close. "These look expensive. Seems a shame to use them just for the wagon."

"They're not just for the wagon." Wade walked up on her other side and captured her gaze again, the heat from his bare chest radiating on her shoulder. "We can use Sage and Daisy for the other vehicle as well. I've also got calls in about some older Arabians and a couple quarter horses to get you started for trail rides."

She took the opportunity to turn her back on Harper. "That sounds like a good plan."

Harper stepped around her to be part of the conversation. "Arabians don't have the best reputation."

Wade turned his attention to the sheriff. "Maybe not as a sport horse but a good "dead broke" Arabian is excellent for a novice rider at a resort like this for trail riding and it looks impressive to people who are not familiar with horses."

God, Wade not only sported the best pair of shoulders this side of the Mississippi, but his knowledge about his profession was too attractive to ignore. She always fell for men who knew their stuff, which was why she'd been such an idiot with her ex-husband, the financial planner.

Harper wasn't convinced. "Maybe, but—"

"So, Sheriff, was there anything you needed?" She'd had enough. "I need to discuss plans with Wade right now, but I want to make sure you are all set first."

Harper's irritation at being interrupted in what was sure to be another challenge to Wade that he would lose, quickly changed into a warm smile. "Now that you mention it, I was thinking of chatting with your security guard. Make sure he had my personal number in case anything happens out here. He's barely a man and I'm sure he would like to know he can get manly advice if he needs it."

She had the absurd urge to bat her eyelashes like an helpless Old West flirt, and say "much obliged" but settled for a quick nod. "That is very nice of you. You can take my cart and see if Powell is awake yet. He's in the third to last casita against the ridge."

"I will do that…Kendra." Harper beamed before he gave Wade a hard stare and strode toward the golf cart.

Once Harper had headed down the path, Wade laughed. She turned at the sound and her breath caught in her chest. The honesty of his emotion wriggled its way under her skin and toward her heart.

"Is he always so obvious?"

She nodded. "Oh yes, he definitely doesn't like you."

"Yup, and he definitely likes you."

"I know." She sighed. "He's not a bad guy, but he isn't my type."

Wade's smile disappeared. "What is your type?"

She turned away to study the grooming tools on the table he'd set up. "I like a man who respects me and what I have accomplished and doesn't judge me or try to make me depend on him. I also have no tolerance for know-it-alls. There's nothing wrong with being ignorant of a specific subject." She picked up a rubber object that had a circular pattern of nubs protruding from it and turned toward him. "For example, I have no idea what this is."

He stepped closer. "It's a curry comb."

"What's it for?"

"It's to dislodge dirt from the horse's coat so it can be brushed away."

She held the comb out to him. "See, I don't need to pretend I know everything to run this resort. I just need to hire experts like you to work for me. I'm sure I'll learn a little along the way."

When his hand touched hers, her skin tingled, sending tiny pinpricks up her arms.

He held on to her. "I can teach you anything you want to know."

She looked up into his brown eyes at that and forgot what she'd been about to say. He gazed at her as if she were a jackpot and he couldn't wait to rake her in. God, he made her want to melt, forget her hard-earned lessons about not straying to the other side.

He pulled the comb from her hand and set it back on the table. "You said you wanted to talk to me about plans?"

She needed to focus. Why had she come out here after three days of successfully avoiding him, besides to ditch the sheriff? She took a step back and shifted her gaze to Sage to put her thoughts in order. "Yes, I wanted to know if you have a sister who could help me with something?"

"With what?"

This was a bit awkward. She walked back to Sage to put more space between them before facing him again. "I need to buy some western wear. I've set up certain expectations for this resort with the western motif and I want to see that carried through when we have guests. A t-shirt and jeans are not exactly western wear."

"Actually, they are." He held up his hand as she was about to interrupt. "But I do understand what you mean. I would be happy to help you."

"You?"

He lowered his brows. "Yes, me. My family has been in Arizona for generations. I not only have two sisters, but female cousins, a mother and believe it or not, a few past girlfriends. I'm more than qualified to decide what western wear looks good on a woman."

She flushed at the thought of him studying her in a new outfit, but it would make it a lot easier than having to meet one of his family members. She'd been hesitant to ask as it wasn't very professional. But since he was her employee, it could fall under that line in his job description of "other duties as assigned."

He strolled past her and stroked Sage, making Kendra jealous he wasn't doing it to her.

"We could take a day and drive into Scottsdale. You could try on a number of outfits, see what you feel the most comfortable in."

Her mind spun at the idea. He would pick out clothes he'd like to see her in. She would be undressing in the dressing room and showing him how they looked. What if she needed help with a blouse that buttoned up the back? What if he wanted her to try on a sexy teddy? "No." She shook her head and reined in her imagination. "No, I don't have time to go anywhere. I can buy items online and have them sent next day."

He paused and stared at her. "Wow, I've never known a woman to turn down a shopping trip for clothes."

She shrugged. "Now you do."

"So then, how do you want me to help you with your clothes?"

He could pull her shirt up over her head, or unzip her jeans. Ugh, she needed to stay on task. "We can do it online. If you come to my office after dinner, we can shop then. I don't want to leave this until the last minute."

Wade left the horse and moved closer. He reached into her hair.

"What are you doing?" She pulled away, but didn't get far, as his other hand grasped her arm.

"Whoa, hold on. You have a bird feather in your hair. It will be hard to picture you in a hat with that."

She stilled and let him sift through her hair, his hands gentle as he untangled the feather without dislodging her hair clip. It was far too stimulating.

He held it up. "Got it."

She stepped away quickly. "Thank you. That must have been from the bird's nest I found in the chimney this afternoon."

He contemplated the black- and white-speckled feather. "Hmm, then I think I will keep this as a souvenir."

For some reason, that seemed romantic. She really needed to get her head back in the game. "No sooner do I have the plumbing fixed and up to code then I have to call a chimney sweep. I guess this is what managing a resort is all about."

"I wouldn't know, but it does seem like this place has had a lot of problems." His brow furrowed.

"Yeah, I know. Luckily, none have been insurmountable." She unclipped her hair, quickly brushing her fingers through it to remove any other debris and then wound it back up. "I think it's just part of creating a new oasis in a desert, so to speak."

Wade's eyes turned almost black, which sent excitement skittering down her spine.

"Will you be wearing your hair down once the resort opens?" His voice had lowered and softened, becoming seductive. When he spoke like that she wanted to undress, not talk about work.

She shifted her weight to her right leg. "I hadn't thought about it. Why? Does it matter?"

"It could." Wade studied the feather in his hand again. "You can try my hat tonight and decide."

A shiver of anticipation ran through her, and she covered it by turning away. "Good. And we can talk about my idea for the naked horseback riding." She didn't dare look back at him, but once around the corner she halted. Freak. She gave her golf cart to Harper.

"Would you like this?" Wade's voice had her spinning around.

Damn the man looked good without a shirt. Too good. "And that is?"

"The key to my golf cart."

"No, I can walk."

He strode toward her, his brown cowboy boots hitting the packed desert dirt hard with each step, but her gaze drifted higher to the waistband of his jeans sitting snuggly on trim hips. When he was a few feet away, she lifted her head, trying desperately not to look at the portion of him that made her drool.

"No. Take my cart. I can ride."

"Ride?"

His lips tilted up on one side. "Yeah. I'll give Daisy and Sage a test run with the wagon to come to dinner tonight."

Dinner, right. She couldn't stop staring at his lips. "Okay."

He stepped even closer and took her hand, pressing the key into it. "See you tonight."

She swallowed as he turned and strode back to the stables. When he disappeared around the corner, she took a deep breath. "Shit. Shit. Shit." She was in trouble.

CHAPTER FOUR

"Kendra. Hey, Kendra where are you?" Adriana leaned across the bar and waved her hand before Kendra's face.

She rubbed her eyes. "I'm sorry. I'm a little distracted this afternoon."

"A little?" Adriana pulled her hand back and reached into a cooler behind the bar. Lifting out two Coronas, she used the bottle opener attached to her jeans and pushed one beer across the bar top. "Okay. Spill. And don't give me any crap about being tired or something."

She hesitated, watching the condensation build on the outside of the beer as the desert heat met the chilled bottle. Oh, what the hell. "It's the new stable manager."

Adriana's brows lowered. "If he's giving you problems, I'll be happy to kick his cute butt right off the property."

Kendra smiled inside and shook her head, turning the cold beer around and around with her hand, but not lifting it to her mouth. "No, actually he's an excellent stable manager and he even put Harper in his place."

"I would have liked to have seen that. You sure you don't want me to sleep with the officer? It might cool him off a bit. I doubt he gets much." Adriana winked as she took a sip of beer.

"No. I think the Sheriff is starting to take the hint. At least I hope so."

"So do you need me to do the cowboy? Trust me, that would be a pleasure."

Kendra gripped the Corona bottle tighter. "No." Frowning, she lifted the beer and took a couple swallows. That was the last thing she wanted. But really, what right would she have to forbid it? "Tell me, Adriana, if you find him so attractive, why haven't you approached him? Or have you?"

Adriana shook her head and shrugged, her movement showing off more cleavage in the tight red tank top she wore. "Yes, he's very sexy, but there is something too pure about him. I don't know. I feel like sleeping with him would be to taint him. Does that sound weird?"

"Yes, but I understand what you mean. I didn't think men like him existed in today's world. Not that I know much about him, but yeah, there is something…honorable about him. Not something I'm used to."

"Me neither." Adriana frowned. "So is that the problem? He's too good for us? Because let me tell you—"

Kendra held up her hand. "Hey, slow down, girl. It's nothing like that."

"Then what is it?"

She twirled the bottle again before raising it and taking another swallow. When she lowered the beer, she stared at it. How could she put into words what she felt when she wasn't sure what it was?

"Dios mío, you want him."

She snapped her gaze to Adriana and gave the barest nod.

"Yeehaw! It's about time. He's a hot man. So what's the problem? Isn't he attracted to you?"

Kendra rubbed her eyes again, suddenly sure Adriana would never understand the predicament. "I don't know. I think he might be, but it doesn't matter. Don't you see? I'm his boss. I can't sleep with him. That would show favoritism amongst the employees."

Adriana opened her mouth to speak, but Kendra cut her off. "No, I'm not going to become a perk of working here for all the male employees."

The bartender pouted before taking another sip of beer. "Hey, it was just a thought."

Kendra allowed a small grin to curve her lips. Some people would think her nuts to have hired a former prostitute as a bartender, a former madam as a cook, a current drunk as a landscaper, a hacker as a security guard and a brokenhearted college grad as a bookkeeper, but these were her kind of people. The question was, where did Wade fit into their motley group? At least each of the last stable managers had some flaw. She had yet to find his, unless being perfect was a flaw.

"So let me get this straight. You want the cowboy and think he wants you but can't because he's your employee and that would show favoritism. Is that right?"

She sighed. "Yes. And I can't even sleep at night because all I can think about is him and what it would be like to have sex with him. So I really am tired."

Adriana put her hands on her hips. "First, you don't go to sleep at night anyway. You go to bed in the early-morning hours like me. Second, if you want him that bad, I say go for it. I doubt Billy will be jealous and Powell works at night so how would he know?"

She shook her head. "No, this place is too small and we are too close for me to do that. I'll just have to grin and bear it for the next two months, three weeks and four days." She groaned silently. She couldn't imagine being so close to Wade and not touching him. She stared at her almost empty beer. So this is what was meant by the phrase "crying in your beer." She'd certainly seen her mother do it when her father didn't come home at night, but she'd always given him what for the next morning.

Those nights usually found Kendra at Buddy and Ginger's, learning to play poker. The childless couple lived only three doors down and had always been a safe haven for her...until they'd been forced out of the pathetic excuse of a trailer park. How attracted to her would Wade Johnson be if he knew she'd learned to play poker at the age of seven.

She sighed and looked up, about to take her last couple swallows, when Adriana's expression halted her. The woman's smile reminded Kendra of Wile E. Coyote when he thought he had the Road Runner in his sights. Nothing good ever happened for that damn coyote. "Adriana, what are you thinking?"

The sudden innocent look thrown her way did nothing to dispel her concerns. She lowered her voice to be more stern. "Adriana. Tell me."

Her bartender threw back the rest of her beer and set the bottle down on the bar with a thud. "Just leave it to me and follow my lead tonight."

Kendra shook her head and jumped off the barstool. "No. You behave yourself and I will too. Forget it." Grabbing her beer, she turned and stalked to her office.

That Adriana hadn't pouted made her very uneasy. Kendra's best bet was to stay away from her. Maybe then she could avoid whatever plans were spinning in that hot woman's head.

~~~~~

Wade left the kitchen with a covered plate of food. He'd bet his favorite chaps Kendra hadn't eaten anything yet. The woman certainly wasn't afraid of manual labor or getting dirty. At dinner he heard she'd put together a bookcase in her own casita. That didn't fit with someone who could afford to build a resort unless she had investors. Maybe that was why she was so driven, anxious to open. He, on the other hand, wasn't thrilled at the idea of leading naked people on trail rides.

"Taking another midnight snack?"

Wade shrugged as he strolled up to Powell, the nighttime security guard. "Maybe." Wade wasn't sure how the young man could protect the property. He was thin as a mesquite branch and his gun pulled his pants down.

Powell readjusted the baseball cap with "security" printed on it, his blond hair sticking out an inch all around it. "I don't know how you do it. I've been trying to butter-up Selma for six months now, but she never offers me a plate for while I'm on patrol."

"Maybe you should try asking her."

Powell's eyes widened. "Damn, you know I think you're right. I've never asked her. Thanks."

"No problem. Did the sheriff find you this afternoon?"

"Huh?" Powell looked away. "I guess not. I was still sleeping." He met Wade's gaze. "Need that sleep if I'm going to stay alert all night, you know?"

"I prefer the mornings myself."

"Not me." Powell stood a bit straighter. "I've always been a night person, like the boss. I figure that's an asset in the law enforcement business."

Wade moved the covered plate to his other hand to avoid burning himself. Selma had heated the dish in the oven when she heard the food was for Kendra. "Do you want to be a policeman?"

"I kind of already am. I mean, doing security here. Plus, I've applied for the police academy. I figure this job will help me get in."

"So you'll leave here if you're accepted?"

Powell flushed, hitching up his pants. "Well yeah, but, well, it can take months, years to get in and I still may not make it. Anyway, I need to get to work. Good night."

"Good night." Wade watched Powell climb into his golf cart and head down the road toward the creek bed. He doubted very much the man would ever be accepted into the academy. He didn't have the confidence or the presence. Shaking his head, Wade continued toward Kendra's office.

He'd been thinking about her all afternoon. Although she'd kept her composure with Harper around, he'd seen that look of wanting in her eyes again when he'd brushed the horses. He'd had to take a deep breath as sharp sexual need raced through his body.

If she could show such strong emotion when his shirt was off, what made her so stoic the rest of the time? His grandmother used to say still waters ran deep, and for the first time he could associate that with a person.

He rapped twice on the door and entered. As he expected, her eyes were focused on the computer screen. She hadn't even heard him knock. "Time for dinner."

"What? Oh, already?"

He shook his head. "It's after eight."

She looked at her screen again. "Guess I'll grab a shake."

Setting the dish of food on the table, he strode to her desk and rolled her in her chair to the space beside the computer. Then he piled up the papers and moved them to the edge of the desk.

"What are you doing?"

"I'm making you eat your dinner. Selma prepared it especially for you." He placed the covered plate in front of her and pulled the fork and knife wrapped in a napkin out of his back pocket. "Here. Now eat."

She stared at the food as if she'd never seen such a thing before finally really looking at him. Her eyes were wide. "No one has ever brought me my dinner. Thank you."

Something in her gaze had him swallowing a lump in his throat. When she'd said "no one," she'd truly meant it. That simple statement was too heartbreaking to contemplate. So he pretended she hadn't just revealed a significant piece of her life and grabbed a chair from her table. He placed it next to her, which put him directly in front of her computer and dropped his hat on her desk.

Quickly, he minimized all seven of her screens and opened her browser. "You eat while I find the websites we need for you to go shopping."

She gazed at him with that unreadable look of hers as she chewed. After she swallowed, she nodded. "Thanks." She turned back to her food, practically shoveling it in her mouth like a man who'd been out on the range all day. No wonder the woman was so thin. She didn't stop working to eat.

Forcing himself to look at the computer instead of the attractive woman sitting next to him, he pulled up a few websites he liked then closed one. No need to overwhelm her with choices. Some women would try on every dress in their size to be sure they'd left no stone unturned. His twin cousins were like that and they were only seventeen.

Glancing at Kendra, he caught her expression of bliss as she bit into Selma's giant biscuit. He'd slathered butter on it, and a drop of the warm, salty liquid dribbled along the corner of Kendra's lip. Even as his groin tightened at the sight, her tongue came out to lick it clean.

Stifling a groan, he whipped his gaze back to the screen. Shopping was much safer than watching his boss eat. Clicking on the women's section of the two sites, he quickly had a dozen outfits chosen. Nothing too frilly. That wasn't her. Everything he'd chosen edged toward ranch owner and less toward innocent farm girl. Everything except one outfit that would be a fantasy for him, just to see her reaction.

"Okay, I'm ready to shop." Kendra wiped her mouth on the napkin he'd brought then picked up the dirty dish and set it on her table.

He stood and pulled out the chair he'd been using. "I've picked out a dozen or so for you to look at. I'm not sure what your price range is, so if it's too much, we can probably find something cheaper on other sites, but I need to know what you like."

She hesitated before the chair and he sensed nervousness, yet her expression showed nothing. Was he starting to read her in other ways?

"I appreciate it." She sat and he pushed her chair forward. Her hands grasped the desk as if she'd been surprised by the movement. Hadn't she had her chair pushed in for her before? His curiosity was piqued.

In no time she was perusing his choices. Unlike most women he knew, she didn't ooh and aah over the clothes. Instead, she appeared to analyze each one, zooming in on pictures, scrutinizing the skirt lengths. Every skirt that ended mid-calf or higher she closed out.

When she came upon the jeans he'd chosen, she stopped. "Do you really think it would be appropriate to wear jeans?"

"I do. It may not be what you want to greet your guests in, but if you decide to go riding with them, or if you are having a barbeque with them, it would be fine."

She reviewed the three pair he'd chosen and closed out one. Her faith in his judgment stoked his pride. Then she clicked on his fantasy outfit. She'd never wear it, but he couldn't wait to see her reaction.

She stared at the low-cut, white frilly top with no sleeves that ended just beneath the model's breasts. The matching skirt barely covered the woman's ass. He grinned.

"Perfect." She turned and looked up at him. "I think I should wear this the first day the resort is open."

"What?"

She turned back to the screen. "Absolutely. I wish there were more like this one. Are there?"

He lowered his brows at the thought of her greeting her guests in that outfit. Shit. "Uh, I'm not sure that would be such a good idea. It wasn't really the occasion I was thinking."

"Then when?" She zoomed in on the top, making the woman's breasts appear huge.

He swallowed hard. "I thought that outfit would be more suitable for a private visit. Say, if you had someone special over for dinner." His blood heated at being caught. No matter what, he refused to tell her it was something he'd love to see her in.

He sat down in her office chair and studied her. She tried to hide it, but he noticed the hint of a grin on her face. She was *teasing* him.

"I definitely have to buy this one."

"If you do, I will hold you to modeling it for me, just to make sure it fits right."

She faced him then in surprise, but he couldn't hold his smirk.

She laughed and the picture disappeared. "That's not going to happen. But I do like these other ones. I'll order them."

Wade's heart tripped at her laughter. Her whole face changed, making her downright breath-stopping.

"Oh damn, I'm going to need cowboy boots, right?"

She faced him again and he attempted to focus. "Yup, and a hat too."

"That's right. You said you wanted me to try yours."

He did? He didn't remember that. He'd never let anyone wear his hat. He must have looked confused because she nodded.

"Yes, you said I should try it with my hair down." She reached up and unclipped the mass of dark waves.

His heart started to beat double time. It took all his willpower not to grab her to him and kiss her, burying his hands in her long, curly strands. Her hair transformed her usually stern face into that of a confident siren. Someone he could envision on top of him, her hair brushing his face as she leaned over him.

"Wade?"

He shook himself. "Yeah."

"I can't try it on unless you give it to me."

"Right." He handed her the black felt hat. "Always handle the hat at the brim, not the crown."

"Okay." She set it on her head. Again, though her expression was bland, he sensed she was anxious about this.

She had nothing to be anxious about. Despite the hat being far too big, she looked hot. His blood revved, his balls tightened and his body heated. The last thing he needed was for her to be sauntering about looking good enough for a roll in the hay. Best to be truthful. "That look is more for an evening out. I'm not sure it's as businesslike as you want. Why don't you put your hair up and try it?"

She nodded once and placed his hat on her desk. Scooping up her hair again, she twirled it around and clipped it. He could imagine her doing the same thing after sex and he had to adjust his position in the chair to make room for his growing erection.

Depositing the hat on her head, she turned expectantly to him. "How about now?"

Shit, the woman was sexy no matter what, but at least this way he could hold on to his control a bit more. "That's better. The problem is hats and boots really have to be tried on to find the right size."

She took his hat off and carefully handed it back to him. He willed himself not to inhale her scent on it before dropping it back on the desk.

"I can always order a couple of each and whatever doesn't fit I can send back. I need to have everything before next week."

The woman obviously had no worries about money. As soon as his three months were up, he would breathe a lot easier too. He'd have a good deposit stashed away for a piece of land and he would have fulfilled his obligation to Dale…that is if he stopped ogling the boss and started questioning the employees. From what he'd witnessed so far, everyone here was loyal to her. What would she think if she found out his job at Poker Flat was twofold and included spying on her? His stomach tightened, a feeling he didn't like at all.

"Could you find a few you think would work?"

Find what? What were they talking about? "Probably. Do you have anything particular in mind?"

She cocked her head and stared at him. Shit, had he made any sense?

"I think I'd like a hat that is not as heavy as yours, but I'm clueless about boots."

Hats and boots. Right. "Sure, let me see."

She stood and moved the chair she'd sat in back to the table, so he wheeled her office chair in front of the computer and pulled up two hat and two boot styles, one for jeans and one for dresses. That reminded him she'd deleted all the short-skirt options. Another interesting fact about Miss Kendra Lowe.

She stood behind him, her body heat seeping through his shirt and warming his shoulder.

"I like those." She pointed to the pair of plain black women's boots he'd selected for casual wear. They had simple stitching and came almost to the knee.

Her almond-rose scent followed her arm movement and it took all his control not to take her hand and set it against the growing bulge in his pants. "I'll let you order your size."

"What about the hat size?" Her arm withdrew, but her hand rested on his shoulder, causing his light cotton shirt to suddenly feel far too warm.

He took a deep breath. "That's a good question." He looked up at her and despite her control over her features, he could feel her leaning toward him, her body sending off signals she wanted to be close. It was far more than he could withstand.

He rose, pushed the office chair out from between them and cupped her head at the back of her neck. The minute he touched her soft skin and silky hair, his path was set. Gently, he moved his hands to her crown, as if approaching an unbroken colt. He lowered his voice. "I'd say you are about a seven and an eighth. I would suggest getting that size and one larger to accommodate your hair up like this." He couldn't have resisted touching the clump of hair on the back of her head even if someone promised to give him a ranch if he didn't. Without questioning himself, he unclipped the dark mass and ran his hand through it. Its soft waves flowed through his fingers like water around the rocks in a creek.

She gazed up at him and her face changed. His cock hardened as desire flooded her features.

He found his hand grasping the back of her head, tilting her face. He smoothed his other down her back and pulled her closer. Her intake of breath at his movement was the only encouragement he needed. Lowering his face, he softly brushed her lips.

The smallest of noises came from the back of her throat. He couldn't stop. He craved more.

Kendra melted into Wade when his tongue breached her lips and swept inside her mouth. His strong gentleness caused ripples of wanting to echo throughout her body. She grasped his neck, pressing herself against him. Her hips moving against his, pushing against the hard bulge beneath his jeans.

He cupped her ass and his kiss became more demanding. He wanted total surrender, but that wasn't going to happen.

A knock on the door jerked her from her sexual haze. Pulling away, she stepped to the side of Wade's strong body and faced the door, heat flooding her cheeks. What had she been thinking?

"Hey, Kendra, I think you need a break by now." Adriana burst in before halting at the sight of her and Wade.

He still faced the back wall of her office, while she looked squarely at her bartender. "Actually, I was thinking the same thing. How about a swim?"

Adriana wasn't fooled. That woman could sense sex a mile away. Her lips turned up into a cunning grin. Uh-oh.

"As much as skinny dipping sounds like a great idea—"

"Wait, who said anything—"

"Billy said he had to add more chemicals to the pool after the designers finally finished the waterfall today, so we have to wait."

Adriana looked smug, as if that was exactly what she wanted. Never a good sign.

Wade finally turned around, Kendra's computer hiding the still-substantial bulge in his jeans. "I'll let you two take your break. I need to get up early tomorrow. I have two more horses being delivered." He donned his hat, ready to leave.

Adriana eyed him like he was a chocolate lollipop and she would lick him down to the stick. "Oh no, we need you to play too. Otherwise there's no game."

Kendra tensed. "Adriana, what are you talking about?"

The curvy bartender held out a deck of cards. "Poker."

Ah, whatever Adriana had in her head if it involved poker, there would be no problem.

Wade's eyebrows lowered. "Poker? Are we betting? I'm not a big one for winning or losing hard-earned money."

Kendra stiffened. That certainly put her in her place. "Guess that settles that. Anyway, I should probably order these items." She pulled her office chair back to her desk. When she glanced up, Adriana was shaking her head, a giant smile on her face.

"We're not betting money. We're betting clothes. Anyone 'up' for strip poker?"

Wade grinned, turning to Kendra. "I haven't played that since I was sixteen." He wiggled his brows at her like he expected to win. He did know she'd been a professional poker player, didn't he? His confident smirk was too challenging to pass up. If he thought he would get her clothes off that easily, he was in for a surprise. She looked back at Adriana. "I'll deal first."

"Uh-huh. It's my idea, I make the rules. We play five card draw, deuces and one-eyed jacks wild."

Kendra silently groaned. She hated wild cards. Any self-respecting poker player did.

Wade stepped up to the table and held out a chair. "Sounds good to me."

Adriana quickly slipped into it and shuffled. Wade moved to another chair and held it out for Kendra.

"Thank you." She could get used to being treated like a queen.

Wade tipped his hat before sliding into the seat next to her. The round table had four chairs, but the empty chair sat between Wade and Adriana.

Adriana pushed the deck toward Wade to cut. "Okay, no cheating and no ante. But if you want to stay in, you must bet one piece of clothing after the deal. After the draw, you can bet as many as you want."

Kendra studied Adriana. "You've done this before, haven't you?"

"Maybe." She winked and dealt the cards.

CHAPTER FIVE

Adriana reached behind her and unhooked her bra. Kendra tensed. She should have known her bartender would lose faster than a rattlesnake after a rabbit. It appeared in so doing, Adriana would win Wade, and there was no policy about employees dating. Something she should probably rectify in the morning.

"Wow, you two are good." Adriana slipped the straps down her arms and threw the lace pink bra onto the pile of clothes on the floor next to her. "This hand could be my last. All I have left is my thong and my bracelet."

Wade looked at Adriana's full, dusky breasts and smiled, then turned back to Kendra. "I believe it's your deal. I'm betting you're going to lose this next hand."

She took the cards from him but missed a few as his index finger brushed her palm. Gathering up the loose cards, she then shuffled, refusing to look at him. The man was too much temptation, especially sitting next to her, bare-chested, in nothing but his hat and jeans. He'd even lost his belt. Did he wear underwear?

She'd been doing fine until he'd taken off his shirt. Then her concentration had gone south. She lost two hands, one because she forgot deuces were wild and another because she'd discarded a one-eyed jack to make her draw. Her shoes and socks were now sitting next to her on the floor, and she was trying not to keep glancing at the light line of hair running down Wade's hard chest.

Keeping her eyes averted from him, she dealt and studied her cards. Two queens, a deuce, a ten and an ace. Now to remember to keep the deuce.

Adriana opened the bet. "I'll stay in with my bracelet."

Wade smiled. "I'll bet my hat."

"And I'll bet my hair clip to stay in. Adriana, how many cards do you want?"

"I'll take three."

She really didn't care for playing recreational poker. She just couldn't get used to it. She dealt three cards and watched as Adriana lifted them. She had something, but not much based on her facial reaction.

"Wade?"

"I'm good."

She studied his face. He simply grinned at her as he had for every hand. The man was good at hiding what his cards brought him. She'd give him that. But he wasn't good with strategy. Her gaze moved to his chest and the definition of his distinct pectoral muscles. She wanted to touch them in the worst way.

"Kendra? Are you taking any cards?" Adriana's voice snapped her attention away from Wade.

She quickly reviewed her hand again. Putting down the ace and ten, she picked up two more cards. A ten and another queen now sat in her hand. She looked expectantly at Adriana.

"I'll bet my thong."

Kendra sighed inside. What would Wade think when Adriana lost? Would he want to stop the game? Escort the naked beauty back to her room? It would probably be for the best. But even at that thought, Wade's searing kiss came back to haunt her, and her stomach plummeted.

"I'm going all-in." Challenge rang clear in Wade's voice.

"Woo hoo!" Adriana winked at him. "So what does all-in mean? How many pieces of clothing are you betting?"

He grinned. "The three I have left."

Adriana pouted. "Are you sure you want to do that? You do know Kendra was a professional poker player, right?"

Wade lost his smile. He turned away from Adriana and stared at her. "Is that true?"

She didn't like the defensive feeling growing in the pit of her stomach. She may be ashamed of her trailer trash childhood, but she was damn proud of her success as a poker player. She didn't break his gaze. "Yes, I was. And I was good."

Adriana piped in. "Yeah, just look at this resort. Only the Night Owl could make this a reality."

"The Night Owl?" Wade frowned. "What's that?"

Kendra spoke before Adriana could continue. "That's what the announcers started to call me. It was because the later into the night the hands went, the sharper I became. The name stuck. I was called Night Owl Lowe."

Wade glanced at Adriana, who nodded enthusiastically. She lifted one brow, her doubt about his hand clear. "So are you sure you want to go all-in?"

He turned and studied Kendra. She could see him contemplating what he should do. Then he gave her a seductive smile that promised her every sexual joy she desired and she forgot to breathe.

"Yeah, I'm all-in."

Her heart sped and she took in much-needed air. She glanced at her cards, careful not to give away her hand. Unless he had four kings, four aces or five of a kind, she would soon see him naked. What if he won? What was she willing to lose? Not her jeans. She didn't want him to see her left leg. "I'll bet my tank, my belt and my bra."

His eyes widened before his gaze dipped to her chest. She couldn't help taking a deep breath as excitement raced through her. For the first time playing poker, she almost wanted to lose.

"Well, I'm going to have to fold. Too daring for me." Adriana pushed back her chair. "I might as well go to bed. It's getting late and I have to meet the beer delivery truck tomorrow. Let me know who won." She scooped up her clothes and headed for the door.

Kendra pulled her gaze from Wade. "Wait. You're practically naked. Don't you want to dress before you go?"

"Why?" Adriana winked. "This is a nude resort and I'm not on the clock. I might as well practice." Laughing, she exited the office, pulling the door shut behind her.

Kendra glanced at Wade and swallowed. "We can quit if you like."

"Oh no, I'm seeing this hand through."

She sighed. "Then I call."

Wade laid down his cards. "Full House."

Exuberance over her win shot through her even as a tinge of disappointment followed. She laid out her cards. "Four queens."

"Shit." Wade studied her cards. "Mine is a great hand, a natural. I should have won."

She agreed. "If we were playing real poker that *would* be a great hand."

He looked at her with admiration. Avoiding his gaze, she leaned forward to swoop his cards into the deck, but he stopped her hand with his own. "Aren't you forgetting something?"

She shrugged as she stared at his large, warm hand covering her own. "You don't have to strip. We can just say I won the night."

"Not a chance. I always pay my debts."

She glanced up to find him far more serious than the game called for. Then he smirked. "Besides, it's not every day I take my clothes off for a beautiful woman."

If he kept talking like that, she'd soon be shedding her own clothes.

Wade stood. After taking off his hat, he set it on the table then ran his hand through his hair a couple times. And he had hair worth running hands through. As he undid the button of his jeans, she found herself gripping the deck of cards like a lifeline and forced herself to drop them on the table.

Wade unzipped his pants and with little ceremony pushed them down, showing he wore the simple white briefs she'd expect from him. Stepping out of his jeans, he neatly folded them and added them to the pile of his clothes on the chair next to him. Her gaze riveted to his sinewy thigh muscles as they moved.

Then he faced her. His cock pushed against his underwear, causing her throat to close. He didn't continue, and she moved her gaze from his crotch to his face.

He no longer smiled. His eyes had grown almost black as he focused on her. "I wouldn't do this for just anyone, Kendra."

She swallowed hard.

His lips curved up in the barest of smiles that held more heat than the Sonoran desert in mid-July. He moved his hands to the waistband of his briefs, and she licked her lips, anxious to see his cock revealed.

He stilled. "You can't do that and expect me to continue on alone. I'll need your help."

Wade's balls tightened as Kendra's gaze remained on his hidden cock. The game hadn't gone as he'd planned, but it certainly had turned out to his advantage. Who knew losing could be so satisfying?

He tilted her chin to look at him. "I think you better take over."

"You want me to take them off?"

He nodded, his body tensing at her question.

She stood, her gaze still on his underwear. His cock jerked of its own accord as if it knew it would soon be free.

Lifting her face, she stared at his chest and tentatively touched him there with both hands. Her eyes closed as his nipples hardened beneath her palms.

Instinct kept him from grasping her to him. Her position as his boss might stop her and right now he didn't give a shit about their positions, except maybe the position he'd like to enter her in. He was too hard to think beyond diving inside her and making her come…if she let him.

Her eyes opened and her hands moved. She learned his chest like a blind person, feeling every contour, touching each mound and valley. It took all his control to stand there and not touch. As she moved downward over his abdominals, he tensed reflexively and her intake of breath told him she liked his movement.

Finally, she reached his underwear and dipped her fingers just inside the waistband. His cock hardened even more, painfully. He took a deep breath, not wanting to spook her, but her almond-rose scent filled his nostrils and he couldn't stop from grasping her shoulders.

She didn't appear to notice as she maneuvered his last barrier past his hips and over his cock, allowing it to spring free.

His control returned as she worked the briefs down his legs until he stepped from them. But when she remained kneeling on the floor, he gritted his teeth. The possibilities of what she could do from there caused his heart to race.

Her hands skimmed up his legs and over his thighs before she cupped his balls in one hand and dropped a featherlight kiss on his dick.

He groaned at the touch of her lips. If only—

Kendra's mouth opened and she sucked in his cock to the sensitive ridge that circled the head.

Shit yes. She lightly bit, just enough to send shards of need straight to his balls.

At the soft moan she gave, which vibrated his tip, he opened the clip on the top of her head and buried his hand in her hair. It took all his strength not to push her face closer to allow him deeper access to her warm, wet mouth.

As if she were a mind reader, she grasped his base and took him farther inside until he hit her throat.

"God, that feels good."

In response, she moved her mouth up and down, stroking her tongue along the underside of his cock. His muscles tensed with need, but he wanted her to need too.

Bending slightly, he pulled her tank top up and she released him to lift her arms but quickly reconnected to suck him hard. Once her arms were free, she grasped his thighs and pulled him closer into her mouth, even deeper.

He closed his eyes, reveling in the sensations of her tongue and teeth. He would not come. No matter what. Not until she had her pleasure. Opening his eyes, he looked down to see her large breasts in a practical black bra, smashed against his legs. Reaching behind her, he unhooked the closure, anxious to touch her bare skin.

When she pulled back to his tip, he cupped both breasts and rubbed his thumbs against her taut nipples.

Her teeth drew tighter around his head.

Gently, he cupped her breasts and pulled her upward.

She moaned as his cock broke from her lips. "You taste so good."

Pre-cum leaked from his tip at her words. Shit, he couldn't hold on much longer. Hooking his chair with his leg, he sat and pulled her toward him. "I want to taste you too."

Cupping a breast, he licked at the hard nipple before sucking in the nub. Releasing it, he licked it again.

Her hands gripped his shoulders. "Yes. Please."

Happy to oblige, he moved to the other breast, giving it the same treatment as his fingers found the wet nipple of the other.

Kendra pushed her breasts toward him, hungry for his touch. Shit, he wanted her now. He used both hands to undo her jeans.

With help from her, they wriggled them down to her knees before she stopped him.

He stilled. She wouldn't end it now, would she? He looked up and she met his gaze.

"Let me."

He wasn't sure what she meant, but he would do anything for her right now.

Steadying herself by holding his shoulder with her left hand, she pulled her right leg from her jeans and panties, leaving them partially on her left leg. He hoped that meant she couldn't be bothered to shuck all her clothes when his hard cock was waiting to be sheathed.

"Do you have protection?"

His heart started beating again. That, he had. Grabbing his jeans off the pile, he dug into his wallet and pulled out the single condom he kept for unexpected encounters. He'd never needed it before now. Silently thanking his older brother for the tip, he ripped open the package and quickly sheathed himself. He pulled her closer by the hips until she straddled him. "Tonight, you ride."

Her lips quirked, an unusual occurrence. "Are you willing to go all-in?"

He could smell the scent of her readiness and his cock throbbed with the need to be inside her. "Of course. Cowboys never fold."

"Good to know." With that, she bent her knees and lowered herself, just far enough for his cock to breach her entrance.

Wade lost his grin as the feel of her very tight pussy surrounded his head. He squeezed her hips. "Shit, you feel great."

"So do you, but you're very large."

"Take your time. There's no rush." He should have offered to stop, but he couldn't. The best he could do is let her set the pace, a pace that was already disintegrating his control.

She continued her descent until he was squeezed fully inside her then she sat still.

He let her adjust to his body. His dick was significantly wide and she was so small her sheath gripped him hard. He cupped her breasts and scraped his teeth across both hard nipples. Her head fell back as she arched into him. He took a chance and nibbled on each one, biting first the tip and then sucking it into his mouth.

Her hips reacted in response and tilted backward and forward, her clit brushing against the hair between his legs. The motion pulled at his cock and he couldn't stop from lifting his hips, pressing himself deeper, as he feasted upon her rosy nipples.

Her movements turned stronger and faster as she ground herself against him. She panted, her hands gripping his shoulders as she lost herself in the hard mating of their bodies. His cock drank in the friction of her wet pussy and he glanced up to see her face tight with pleasure. The sight broke his control.

He grasped her ass, encouraging her as his own need escalated. Her tight sheath sucked at him while her hips moved, pulling at his cock, demanding his release. It was too much to resist.

Her moans grew louder, higher pitched until her scream rent the air and her pussy pulsed against his cock. His seed exploded from him, pumping from him in satisfying spurts. His body rocked hers and eventually her moans softened to whimpers.

Wrapping his arms around her, he buried his hand in her hair and kissed the side of her head as her forehead rested on his shoulder. Her panting was still harsh from her orgasm.

He hadn't expected that and the reality far surpassed what he'd envisioned alone in his room. She was perfect. Strong, uninhibited and sexy.

She lifted her head and looked at him, her face once again unreadable.

He smiled. "I'd be happy to lose to you any day."

Her eyes did widen slightly then a tiny frown graced her forehead. "Somehow I think you won that one."

He chuckled. "As long as you enjoyed it, I'm good either way."

Her face shuttered once again. "I'd better get back to work."

Work? She was still fully impaled on him and she wanted to work? He kept it light, wanting her to somehow acknowledge what they'd shared. "You can always go for another ride. I don't mind." He winked, wanting to see that freely expressed look of pleasure on her face again.

She shook her head and stood, the pull of her pussy against his cock making him hard all over again. He groaned at the loss of her heat.

While he pulled the condom off and dropped it in the trash next to him, she yanked up her jeans and quickly donned her bra and tank.

He crossed his arms, remaining where he was as he watched her short, quick movements. She acted like no other woman he'd been with and the puzzle of Kendra Lowe, professional poker player, had him intrigued and just a bit ticked off.

She bent to search beneath the table, her jean-clad ass in the air. "Did you see where my hair clip went?"

He didn't say anything, simply waited for her to look at him.

She finally rose and turned. Her face revealed her interest in his naked body before her usual stoic expression took its place. "Wade?"

He shrugged. "I like your hair down much better."

"But you said it wasn't businesslike."

"Exactly."

The slight blush that filled her cheeks told him he made a hit. Good. It wasn't human to be so emotionless.

"Did you enjoy your ride?"

She moved her weight to her right hip. "Yes. Did you?"

Now they were getting somewhere. "Immensely and I would very much like to sink into your body again."

He sensed her interest before she denied them. "I can't. I shouldn't have done that. I'm your supervisor. It's wrong, low class."

Wade stood, her words hurting more than they should. "So you feel like you were slumming to lower yourself to be with me? Fine. Just remember, next time you want a quick fuck, don't come looking for me. When I have sex with a woman, it's not just about our bodies. My mistake."

Slamming his hat on his head, he grabbed up his clothes and strode to the door.

"Wade. That's not what I meant."

He grabbed the handle and pulled the door open. Luckily, no one was in the hall as he exited. His anger dissipated as the coolness of the area made him alert to his nudity. Entering the common room, he stopped and listened. No footsteps followed him. He sneered. Of course not, that would mean she cared what he thought. Dropping his boots, he threw on his underwear, jeans and shirt. Then he flopped down on one of the couches and tugged on his boots.

He should have never satisfied his need with his boss. He'd let himself be distracted by her uniqueness, intelligence and unreadable personality. He was better than that. He worked at Poker Flat for a reason. It was time he kept that reason in the forefront of his mind.

Stalking out the main doors, he strode toward his casita. So the woman was a poker player. He'd bet the resort was paid for with her winnings. That was a relief at least. So why did his three predecessors leave?

"Heading to bed?"

Wade halted and waited for the person to move out of the shadows. It was Powell again. "Yup. Long day."

The security guard shook his head. "Mine has barely begun. Have a good night."

Wade hesitated. This was a good time as any to ask some questions. "Hey, did you know the other stable managers?"

"Of course." Powell strolled toward him. "Crandall, Jorge and Michael. They just got younger and younger. You're the youngest. Maybe the boss thought younger would be less likely to argue with her."

"Did she disagree with all three?"

Powell thought for a moment. "Now that you ask, I think Michael and she got along fine. Why?"

Wade shrugged. "Just wondering what I might have to deal with."

"Well, the lady definitely likes things done her way. So if you're fine with that, it should be smooth sailing."

"Thanks. Guess I'll turn in now."

"Yeah." Powell turned away. "Got to do my rounds."

Wade watched the man stroll down the path to the empty guest casitas. So Kendra wanted things her way. That did fit with what he'd seen, and some men had problems taking direction from a woman. Still, that might account for Crandall and Jorge leaving but it didn't answer the question of why Michael left.

He yawned. Spending time with the Night Owl was not conducive to a good night's sleep. Striding down the path toward his own bed, it became clear to him spending time with the boss wasn't conducive to his ego either. Best to let things lie as they were.

~~~~~~

Kendra stared at the wildlife manager in his crisp gray uniform. "What are you talking about? We haven't noticed any bald eagles in this area since I bought the land. If one had made a nest nearby, I certainly would have seen it at some point."

The game official shook his head. "We are simply following up on a reported sighting, ma'am. Now please show us any fireplaces you may have here."

Kendra fisted her hands. Fireplaces? Now why did he specifically ask about fireplaces? Someone must have told him about the nest and junk she found before the chimney sweep arrived. Someone had ratted her out.

After continual problems all week that she'd reasoned away, it became crystal clear someone was sabotaging her. The question was who. Wade's anger of four nights ago came to mind. Could he be that mad at her? She'd tried to see him the next morning to apologize, but he'd already left with Adriana and the wagon to pick up the beer delivery. After that, cracked windows, a leaky roof, and ripped-out watering lines for the lawns had taken her attention.

Lacey stood next to her, her worried look telling Kendra this was no easy matter to sidestep. "Lacey, take this gentleman out to the bar and show him that fireplace."

"Of course, right this way." Lacey, smart girl, led the gentleman back out through the main doors he'd entered and around the building.

Adriana burst in from the bar entrance. "Why is the Game and Fish department here?"

"They're saying we have a bald eagle nest in a chimney. Have you seen any bald eagles?"

Adriana put her hands on her hips. "How would they know we had a bird nest in the first place?"

"Someone told them. Someone who knew." Kendra headed for the large chimney in the common area, Adriana on her heels. She moved the logs stacked in place for the first fire and opened the flue. The chimney was clean. She breathed a sigh of relief. At least no one had blocked it since the chimney sweep had come. She closed the flue and waited.

Adriana wasn't as patient. "We need to find out who did this. Did he say who called him?"

Kendra shook her head. "He said there was a sighting."

"Sighting, my ass. Who knew about the nest you found?"

"Everyone on the property. Even the sheriff and the chimney sweep knew. It could be anyone."

Adriana sat on a nearby couch. "Yes, but not everyone wants this place to close."

"Why would a bald eagle close the resort?"

"Kendra, you spend too much time working. If you got out once in a while you'd know when bald eagles build nests, Arizona Game and Fish don't allow people near them. Last December they closed the entire Aqua Fria river part of Lake Pleasant until June!"

"Half a year?" Nausea threatened her insides. She couldn't afford for her resort to be closed half the year, especially in the winter months when nudists were looking for warmer climates. "I can't close that long."

The side door opened and Lacey walked the officer into the great room. Throwing a worried glance at Kendra, she pointed to the fireplace. "That's the only other large one we have. All the others are very small and are in the larger casitas. I would be happy to show you them."

The officer wrote something on his clipboard then set it down. "It would have to be a very large fireplace. If the others are smaller then I don't need to inspect them." He moved closer to the twelve-foot-wide centerpiece of the resort. "Why are these logs here?"

Kendra answered. "We had them stacked and ready for our first fire, but I moved them so you could inspect it."

He picked up his clipboard again and wrote. Then he opened the flue and peered up the chimney. When he came out, he wrote another note. "These two chimneys have been cleaned."

"Yes. I had them cleaned to prepare for our opening."

He looked at her with a hard stare. "Ma'am, you won't be opening if you disturbed a bald eagle's nest."

Okay, it was time for him to show his hand. "What are you talking about? You said you had a report of a sighting. What does that have to do with my fireplaces and eagle's nests?"

The man lost a bit of his bravado. "The report was of a sighting of an eagle's nest in a chimney."

Damn. "Who called in the report?"

"It was anonymous."

Wasn't that convenient? "Well, as you can see we have no nests in our chimneys."

The man's face grew serious. "That's because you had them cleaned. Perhaps to hide the evidence. I'll need to see your trash."

"You want to pick through our trash?"

"That's what I said, ma'am."

"Fine. Lacey, please show this gentleman where our trash is. And just so you know, officer, we bring our trash to the dump every other day."

The man's jaw hardened but he nodded and followed Lacey out, his clipboard grasped securely under his arm.

Kendra collapsed onto the couch next to Adriana. "At least he won't find anything in the trash."

"Yeah. But I want to know who betrayed you."

"Believe me, so do I."

The front door opened and the sound of cowboy boots hitting the tile floor had her turning her head. Speak of the devil. Short shuffling steps followed.

Wade came around the corner into the great room, his expression worried. "Billy told me Game and Fish are here."

Billy stopped next to Wade, his face flushed. "I tell him, Miss Kendra. He know lots about Arizona laws."

He knows Arizona law, like maybe that bald eagle nests are a reason to close down a resort? The deck was definitely stacked against her new stable manager as far as she could see. "Yes, they are here. Right now an officer is going through the trash. Billy, you've been bringing the trash to the dump every other day, right?"

Billy nodded. "Every bit, Miss Kendra."

"I'm not sure what he expects to find in there."

Wade moved to the fireplace, glancing at the logs she'd moved. "Does he know about the bird nest you found blocking this chimney?"

She studied him. The man was too open with his emotions. She doubted he was the one who tipped them off. "Yes, he does. Someone told him. He's out back searching for evidence right now. He wasn't too happy I'd had the chimneys cleaned."

Wade leaned against the opposite couch. "That's not necessarily a good thing. He will view it as you covering something up."

She sat straighter. "But I was being responsible so we'd have no unwanted fires in them."

Wade shook his head. "Doesn't matter. Game and Fish has a one-track mind and that is to protect the wildlife at all costs. It's a good focus when the danger is real, but I haven't seen a bald eagle while I've been here. It's just not the right environment."

The front door opened and they all fell silent. To Kendra, the officer's shoes hitting the tiled floor sounded like the footsteps of doom. She rose. Why did she want to vomit right now?

As Lacey and the officer came into the great room, Lacey's face said it all. The man carried a garbage bag in his right hand, his ever-present clipboard in the other.

"Ma'am, it appears you were trying to hide this evidence."

"What evidence?"

The man opened the bag in triumph. "That. That is the remains of a bird's nest."

CHAPTER SIX

She didn't move a muscle, but bile rose up into her throat. Why hadn't that been taken to the dump? She glanced at Billy who looked stunned. Someone had set her up. "I think 'remains' is the key word here, officer. It was a dried up nest that was broken apart. I simply threw it where it was supposed to go, in the trash."

The man stood taller. "If this is a bald eagle's nest, we will have to shut this place down and you will be fined, possibly receive jail time."

Kendra wanted to laugh at the absurd mess, but she remained still. If he expected her to confess because of his threats, he was sadly mistaken.

"Officer." Wade stepped up to the coffee table where the nest lay exposed like a testimony of damnation. "May I take a look at the nest? My family have been ranchers here for generations and I'm pretty good with bird identification."

The officer hesitated. "Any official identification will have to be done by our department."

"I understand."

The officer nodded and Wade spread the bag open farther.

Kendra couldn't have moved if she tried. She had no idea what Wade was about, which added to her stress.

Wade's voice was polite and very deferential. "Sir, the reason I want to examine this nest is this chimney, though large, would still be small for a bald eagle nest. Ah." He pointed. "If you look here, you can see there are a few feathers stuck between the twigs. They are striped horizontally in many rows. I believe a bald eagle has a vertical split of two solid colors. Also, in this area of the nest, it appears there is the skeleton of a smaller bird. Based on that, my guess is this was a Cooper's hawk nest. What do you think?"

The officer joined Wade and poked around in the nest with his pen. "It's very unusual for those hawks to build in a chimney, but then again, it's even more unusual for bald eagles." He lifted the nest and pointed. "Ah, there are two tree branches running through this. Either the branches spanned the chimney, which tricked the birds, or more likely the nest was lifted by strong winds and deposited in the chimney."

"So you agree, it is most likely a Cooper's hawk nest?" Wade's face portrayed a respect the officer obviously appreciated.

"I do. But I will still need confirmation from our experts on staff."

Wade stepped back. "Of course."

Kendra took her first deep breath since hearing Game and Fish had arrived. She owed Wade in a big way.

Adriana jumped up. "Oh, I just have to take a photo of this for my sister. It's so exciting."

Huh? Adriana didn't have a sister. What was the minx up to now?

The officer reached for the bag, but Adriana had already snapped a few pictures with her phone. "Can I take a picture of you holding the bag too? My sister so loves a man in uniform."

At Adriana's blatant perusal of his body, the officer straightened, even smiled for her picture.

After she thanked him, he picked up his damn clipboard.

Kendra motioned Lacey to see him out, but he turned and faced her.

"Ma'am, next time you find a bird nest on your property, call Game and Fish immediately. Do you understand?"

"I do."

The man stared at her a minute longer then turned and followed Lacey out.

When the front door closed, Billy whooped and Adriana fell back onto the couch. "Holy crap, that was close."

Kendra silently agreed. "What was the photo taking all about? You don't have a sister."

She shrugged. "Insurance. I didn't want him coming back and telling us the experts found bald eagle feathers in there when clearly there weren't. I also wanted to have his picture so we would know who was crooked in case we never saw him again and they tried to close down Poker Flat."

Adriana's loyalty had Kendra's eyes tearing up and her admiration for her friend grew. "Thank you." She turned and looked at Wade, who watched her. "And thank you. You saved my resort, my dream. I don't know what to say."

He studied her a moment. "If there's no resort than I don't have a job, so it was in my best interest."

He turned to go but she couldn't let him. "Wade, wait. Please."

He stopped, but didn't turn around.

Adriana jumped up. "That's my cue to leave." She hooked her arm into Billy's. "Come on, Billy. I'll buy you a beer."

Kendra waited until her other two employees had gone outside. When the door closed, she swallowed. "I want to apologize."

He finally turned around and faced her. "For what?"

She took a deep breath. "For what I said the night of the poker game. I didn't mean *you* were low class, I meant my behavior was low class. I'm sorry if you thought I meant you."

He studied her, his scrutiny tougher than any player she'd ever sat across from. "Okay." He turned away again and headed for the door.

He wasn't buying it. For some reason, she needed him to. "Wade."

He kept walking.

Kendra had never run after a man in her life, not even her ex-husband when he walked out on her, but she needed Wade to believe her. She caught up with him before he reached the door. "Wade, please. I mean it. I don't want you to think I look down on you in any way. In fact, I admire you. Believe me."

He turned around at that. "Believe you? How can I? I hear the words, but I don't see it. You show no emotion at all." He jerked his head. "But if that works for you as the boss, then fine. I'm just an employee."

"I can't help how I react. I was a poker player for eight years. I learned early on I couldn't hold my emotions inside during games and let them out when I wasn't playing. I had to keep them in all the time. I had to in order to be successful."

Wade shook his head. "This isn't poker. This is life. Your employees are loyal to you for one reason or another, but you give them nothing in return. No smile of appreciation. No laugh at their jokes. No matter what you're feeling inside, it's not communicating outside."

She stared at him. Her people didn't know how much she appreciated them? Hadn't she praised Lacey the other day? Yes, she did, but it was while telling her to get back to her job. She searched her memory for her employees' reactions to her comments. Everyone was hesitant except Adriana. That woman was so full of life, a microburst couldn't put her down.

Insecurities bubbled up inside her, just like when she was younger. She hated that. "Why are you making me feel like shit?"

His face softened. "There. You're concerned and it's showing." He touched her face, his rough hand gentle against her cheek. "You are a very accomplished, smart woman. You just need to let people see how you feel. Don't live your life behind a mask. People want to see the real you."

He stared at her a minute longer then withdrew his hand and left.

She envied his confident stride as he made his way to his golf cart. It was easy for him to show emotion. He was perfect. He hadn't been hurt. His profession hadn't rested on keeping an unreadable façade. His work with horses and other cowboys required a quick smile, a friendly joke, and probably a scowl now and again.

Turning away, she headed out to the bar. She had more important business matters to attend to than how she appeared to her employees.

Adriana had all the beer bottles out on the bar and was swearing up a storm.

Now what? "Adriana, what are you doing?"

The woman stopped muttering to herself and scowled. "Come here and look at this."

She was almost afraid to, but she walked around the bar anyway. Adriana knelt on the rubber runner that ran down the middle of the space and aimed a flashlight at the wall of the bar. "Look."

Kendra stood next to her and leaned behind the cooler that kept the bottled beer cold. The electrical cord had been cut and it wasn't from a rodent. The slice was clean. She was lucky the live wires still plugged into the wall hadn't started a fire. "Don't touch that cord. Let's get this moved away from the wall."

Once they had rolled up the runner, the two of them maneuvered the cooler out from behind the bar.

Wiping her dirty hands on her jeans, Kendra pulled out a barstool and sat. "Are the iced teas cold or is that cord cut too?"

Adriana opened another cooler and pulled out two teas. "Nope, these are still cold. Figures. Billy wasn't happy. Now I owe him a beer." She came around the bar and sat on the barstool next to Kendra. She lifted her tea. "Here's to two steps forward and two steps back."

Kendra shook her head and refused to clink bottles. "I'm not toasting to that. Can we put the beer into the back cooler until this is fixed?"

Adriana shook her head. "No. I have no idea how long that cord has been cut. I haven't gone for a beer in two days. It wasn't until I brought Billy back here to have one that I felt the beers were warm. They'll all have to be trashed. The poor man looked like he was about to cry. I have more stock in the back, but if you have a lot of people coming next week, I'm going to need to put in a new order."

Kendra stared at the wasted money sitting on her bar. She needed to find whoever was doing this. It didn't make sense for it to be any of her employees because they would lose their jobs if the place didn't open. And all of them needed their jobs.

"Aren't you mad?"

Kendra looked at Adriana. "Of course I'm mad. I'm pissed."

"You certainly don't look it. I'm so angry I could smash every one of those bottles. The only reason I'm holding back is because I'm the one who would have to clean up the mess."

"No, believe me, I'm beyond angry. I need to spend money on beer, an electrician, and figure out how we are going to service our first guests with cold beer if I can't get this fixed."

"Well, it would help to see it." Adriana took a gulp of the iced tea.

"What? You too?"

"Me too, what?" Adriana pushed her face forward, her stance threatening.

Kendra slammed her hand on the bar and scowled. "You and Wade want me to show more emotion. You all want to know what I'm thinking." She took a deep breath, her voice rising. "I'm thinking I'm tired of trying to make this resort a go. I'm thinking I should have just bought a little cottage on the beach in Key West and stuffed the rest of my winnings under a mattress." She threw her arm up. "I'm thinking I'm fucking tired of people sneaking behind my back to sabotage my dream. Is that clear enough?"

Adriana stared at her as if she'd grown two horns, a tail and turned red. Then her bartender burst out laughing, clapping her hands. "Good for you. About time you got angry."

Still breathing hard from her rant, she could barely utter a word. "Huh?"

"Honey, you are the kindest woman I know, but talking to you is like talking to the red rock of Sedona. You suck my energy with your lack of reaction. It is so much more satisfying to see you like this."

"Really? You like me yelling?"

"No. But I like you reacting. It's more reassuring to see you really understand what I'm talking about. At first I used to think you weren't paying attention, but as I've known you for years, I did finally figure out you were. But it's so much better when you scowl, or smile, or even cry."

"That's what Wade said."

"I'm sure as a new employee, he's not used to your poker face." Adriana stared as if she were in a trance.

Kendra grumbled. "It seems my poker face is more of a disadvantage in this profession."

"Good point." Adriana eyed her shrewdly. "How do you think your nude guests will feel if you don't give them a smile of welcome or if you are having dinner with them and not reacting to what they say? They may think you disapprove of their lifestyle."

"I don't disapprove of it. It's not my thing, but I want them to have a nice and safe place to enjoy their vacations." She wanted them to feel welcomed not ostracized for wanting to be naked like Buddy and Ginger were.

"Then maybe you can practice a smile or two. In the meantime, I think we need a plan for the bar. When do our first guests arrive?"

"Four days."

Adriana grimaced. "You're going to pay top dollar to get an electrician here in time."

"Do it." Kendra jumped off her seat. "Whatever it takes. We are opening this resort on Saturday."

"You got it, boss." Adriana winked.

Kendra nodded then added a smile. It felt strange, but she could work on it, especially if it would help her business.

Leaving Adriana to make her phone calls, Kendra headed for her office.

Lacey greeted her at the front desk. "Some packages came for you. I didn't have any orders I was expecting, so I put them in your office."

"Great, thanks." She started to leave but stopped. "I don't know how I'd keep everything in order if it wasn't for you." Then she smiled.

Lacey's face lit up and a faint blush stained her cheeks. "It's my pleasure."

Feeling strange, Kendra headed to her office, letting the smile drop. This would take some time. In the meantime, she had a saboteur to find.

~~~~~

Wade guided one of the Arabians into his stall next to the quarter horses he'd obtained a few days ago. "Ace, this is Sam and Buca. You're going to like it here." Closing the stall door, he strode back toward the front of the barn where he had Sundancer tied. Six horses delivered in eight days. Not bad. He'd take Ace out for a ride later this afternoon and start scouting possible trails.

Picking up the curry comb, he brushed down Sundancer. He'd discovered some interesting information about the last three stable managers while searching the office computer. All three had been in the middle of projects, be it the building of the stable, putting up the fences, or researching horseflesh. Up until the day each quit, there was no indication they were unhappy or had a better job elsewhere. That in itself meant something big had to have happened to have them quit.

He'd talked to Selma and Lacey, but neither had had much interaction with the men except at dinner. Like himself, according to the women, the men were excited about running a new stable. So why leave before it was completed?

His chat with Adriana had been a bit more enlightening because she'd slept with Michael. He did love his new job, but he didn't give women much credit and she'd kept it to only the one time. He wasn't her type. But as far as the other two men, they were too old for her tastes.

The only other fact was that all three had quit in the morning, according to Lacey. It was as if they woke up and suddenly decided they couldn't work at Poker Flat anymore. That was too unusual to be a three-way coincidence. His guess was something had happened the night before to spook them off the job.

Wade put the comb down and pulled off his hat and t-shirt. Putting the hat back on, he grabbed up a bottle of water he'd brought out in a small cooler and chugged the rest down. He was about to pick up the comb again when he heard the crunching of gravel.

Stepping toward the stable entrance, he watched as Billy made his way toward him. The older man was an excellent landscaper, but from what Wade had seen, he did go off on drinking binges and based on his stagger, he'd started last night. "Hey, Billy."

Billy grinned widely, showing his missing tooth. "Howdy there, Wade. Whatcha doin'?"

He sighed. This was the second time he'd seen this and he hadn't been at Poker Flat two weeks yet. Did Kendra know? "Come on in out of the sun. I'll get you a water."

Billy barely made it into the barn before sitting down hard on a bale of hay. "Don't mind if I does. No water for me. But if you gots somethin' stronger?" Billy attempted to wiggle his brows, but they became stuck, crunched up into his forehead.

Wade moved to his small cooler and grabbed a couple waters. "Here. Drink this."

Billy took a swallow and spit it out. "Yuck. That gots no taste."

"I don't care. Drink it." Wade pushed the bottle toward the older man's lips.

Billy obeyed but grumbled. "You ain't so easy like the other ones."

His interest caught, he picked up the curry comb and returned to brushing. "Did the last stable managers share a drink with you?"

Billy looked off into the distance. "Yeah. Nothin' wrong with a little after-dinner drink." He leaned forward, almost toppling over before he realized that position wasn't such a good idea. He lowered his voice. "Can't does it at the main bar, you know. Miss Kendra don't like me drinking."

So Kendra was aware. Of course. The question was, did she know Billy was binging so often? "Then where did you drink?"

"At the casita. Yours. Anytime you wanna, I be there." Billy winked three times before pushing his fist against his eye to stop.

"I'll be sure to let you know when I'm in the mood."

Billy slapped his hand down on his knee. "I knows you was a good one. Tolds Powell that too." Billy frowned. "He don't drink. Neither do Selma or Lacey. It fine for them ladies, but a man oughta drink now and again. You builds up a tolera—head for it that way. No one can pull one over on ya. Now Crandall could drink with the best of 'em, but Jorge were a lightweight. I think that why he has that big fight the night before he leave."

Wade stopped combing and studied Billy as the man grimaced at the bottle of water still in his hand. There'd been a fight? He put down the comb and joined Billy, sitting on an adjacent hay bale. "Who did he fight?"

Billy shrugged. "Dunno. But he has a big shiner the next mornin'. Probably could has held his own if he could has held his liquor. He were scrawny but fast. Saw him knocks a board away that falls toward him when they was finishing the roof. Yup, he were fast when he sober."

Wade took the water from Billy. "I want you to think back. Did Crandall or Michael leave with any bruises?"

"Nope." Billy stilled for a moment then shook his head. "Nope, no bruises, but they was mad."

"At what?"

"Dunno. Crandall don't says nothin' when I drives him over to the garage. Michael don't even waits for a ride. He grab a cart and races down the path." Billy laughed. "Not that them things can go very fast or nothin.'"

Wade sat back, his protective instincts kicking into high gear. Someone wanted Kendra to fail. None of the managers had planned on leaving, that much was clear. Someone made a point of getting rid of them. He'd bet his savings the same person was responsible for all the problems on the resort and for Game and Fish showing up.

A snore jarred Wade from his analysis. Billy had fallen forward and was spread out on the stable floor sound asleep. Part of Wade wanted to shake the man straight, but the other felt sorry for him. Who would hire an old drunk? The question made part of the puzzle pieces fall into place. Kendra hired odd characters. In a way, even she was a bit different. Not the usual entrepreneur. The only person who worked at Poker Flat who wasn't odd was Lacey and possibly himself, but he'd been hired by Dale.

It was probably time to share what he'd discovered so far with his friend. Maybe he and Dale could come up with a few working theories he could investigate further. It wouldn't be long before a slew of naked people would be roaming around the property. That in itself could be cause for someone to keep Poker Flat from opening. He wasn't overjoyed at the prospect himself, but Kendra had her heart set on it and she was the boss.

Billy coughed in his sleep. Inhaling hay probably wasn't the best thing for the old man's health. "Come on, let's find you a better place to sleep it off." He pulled the small man up which was far too easy. Hefting him over his shoulder, Wade brought Billy to his air-conditioned office and laid him on the couch. "Have a good nap, my friend."

Washing his hands from combing Sundancer, he grabbed a half dozen of Selma's churros and headed back to the barn. As he closed the door to his office, another golf cart pulled up. Chewing the sweet cinnamon treat, he made his way to the parking area, his interest piqued by the feminine figure in the long skirt climbing out of the cart.

As he drew closer, he smiled. Damn if the woman didn't fit the image of an owner of a western ranch. All she needed now was a horse. He quickened his step, anxious to see why she'd come by after avoiding the stables for two days.

She strode toward him, her poker face firmly in place, but with her hair tucked up under the brim of her brown cowboy hat, she looked too beautiful for him to care. Her shirt was a no-nonsense cotton button down that disappeared into the deep-blue jean skirt that flared at the bottom, showing off the brown Justin boots he'd chosen for her.

When they were almost toe-to-toe, she raised her head and smiled. "Do you like the clothes you picked out?"

Wade's stomach tightened as the warmth of her smile sent heat racing down his spine. That she'd made an effort to express her welcome had his heart paying attention. The depths to this woman were more interesting than he'd imagined.

Her smile faltered at his silence and he quickly tipped his hat. "Ms. Lowe, may I just say that you look downright ravishing today."

The blush that colored her cheeks pleased him, and he bowed slightly, offering his arm. "Perhaps you would care to step into the shade."

She nodded, even as her smile disappeared. It didn't matter. She was trying and he appreciated her more for that.

"What do you have in your hand?" She craned her neck to see.

He showed her as they walked. "Selma's churros. She gave me a batch to keep in the office for when I needed an energy boost."

Kendra stared at them, shaking her head. "You have definitely sweet talked that woman. She hasn't done that for anyone since she arrived here."

As they entered the barn, he led her to the hay bale Billy had so recently vacated. He was glad he'd moved the old man. No need for Kendra to see him passed out.

Once she sat, he joined her, sitting close. "Would you like one?"

"Yes. I haven't tried them yet." She held up her hand as he was about to interrupt. "I know, I know. I just don't get to the dining room that often. I've been busy."

He gave her a stern look. "You work too hard."

She shrugged. "I have to. This place will succeed or fail based on my decisions, my work, and my money. It all rests on *my* shoulders."

"Here." He handed her a couple churros. "With all that, you need to eat a lot more."

She glanced at him from beneath her brim and he grinned, letting her know he was teasing…somewhat.

"Oh, these are really good." She licked the cinnamon off her fingers. "Any chance I could have another?"

"Of course." He'd give her all the ones in his office just to watch her pink tongue on her finger again. "Here." He held the last five out.

"No, no. I just need one."

She picked one and chewed. When she brought her finger up to lick, he caught her hand. "Here, let me do that."

Kendra sucked in her breath as Wade's mouth enveloped her finger. Her flesh tingled at the sight of his tongue licking all the way down to her palm.

When he finished, he tilted her chin. "Did you enjoy that?"

She couldn't meet his gaze. "Yes."

He stood and lifted her up with him. "I couldn't tell. How about this?" He cupped her face and licked at her lips. She opened her mouth, inviting him in, but he only kissed the corners of her mouth.

Pulling away, he gazed at her. "Well?"

She nodded, not sure why he needed to ask.

Taking his hat off, he threw it on the hay bale. Then he wrapped his arms around her, one hand on her back, the other behind her head. Without preamble, his head lowered and his lips met hers, but the kiss was not gentle. His tongue pushed into her mouth to tangle with her own.

Passion, hot and white, seared through her limbs and she grasped his shoulders, pulling herself into him.

He walked her backward until she felt the new wood of the barn wall against her spine, her hat falling to the floor. His kisses became more demanding.

Abruptly, he stopped and studied her. She could barely stand, and yet he appeared unaffected except for his breathing. "Wade?"

He shook his head. Taking her hands from his arms, he pulled them over her head and tied them with a rope.

"What are you doing?"

He didn't look at her, but concentrated on tying the other end of the rope to a peg on the wall above her. "I'm helping you."

She tried to free her wrists, but the rope was secure. Nervousness threatened. "Let me go."

He traced the line of her jaw with his finger until he reached her ear. "No. You have customers coming in a couple days and I'm going to help you react to them. I will use positive reinforcement to get you to express what you feel."

Some of her panic resided as her curiosity took over. "What do you mean?"

His finger moved down the side of her neck to her collarbone. Ripples of anticipation moved from there to her breasts.

"You are not to speak. I will only take my cues by the look on your face. If you appear to enjoy what I am doing to you, then I'll continue. If I can't tell, then I will stop."

"Wait, what if someone comes?"

His finger moved down the neckline of her shirt and stopped at the first button. "I will hear them if you remain quiet. Now stop talking. Focus on what you feel and show me in your facial expression."

Oh God, what she felt was hot. How was she supposed to show him that?

Wade slowly unbuttoned the first three buttons on her shirt, exposing her cleavage. His finger traced the mounds of her breasts down to her bra. He unbuttoned the rest of her shirt to her skirt.

She expected him to touch her again, but instead he yanked the bottom of her shirt out. "Oh."

He stilled and frowned at her. "I said no talking."

"Can't I make noises?"

"No."

There was no way she would be able to keep silent. No way. But the anticipation of exactly how far he would go had her trying.

Unbuttoning the last two buttons, Wade spread her shirt and tucked it behind her. "Don't move."

She frowned at that command and he grinned. "Unless, of course, you want to push your lovely body toward me, then I may make an exception."

She forced her lips to curve upward.

"Good. For that hesitant smile I will continue."

Wade traced his finger along the edge of her white lace bra, something she'd bought along with the western wear. Adriana's feminine lingerie had given her the idea that not all her underthings needed to be plain.

"What do we have here?"

CHAPTER SEVEN

Wade's fingers played with the plastic clip between her breasts and she held her breath. She hadn't known he'd be seeing her like this. She'd ordered the front-clasp bra to try it, not sure it would give her the support she needed. As Wade sprung the clasp, releasing the bra cups to scrape across her nipples, excitement shot down to her pussy, forcing her to breathe again. She needed more of these front clasps for sure.

She couldn't resist watching Wade's finger trace a path from her cleavage to her left breast, where it circled her areola before brushing across her nipple. The pebbled skin showed him exactly how aroused she was, but he looked at her to see her reaction. She smirked, the best she could do. She wanted more. She shouldn't, but his touch had started a tension deep in her sheath and she couldn't resist him.

His smile was full as he brought his attention back to her breast. With the lightest of pressure, he blew on her nipple. Seeing his mouth so close and not touching made her want to grab his head, but her hands were too securely fastened.

He put his finger into his mouth then ran it around her nipple. She sucked in air as tingles of hot yearning spread across her abdomen. His hands came down to grasp her waist, holding her still. His mouth finally clasped her tortured peak. He sucked. Hard. Need burst in her core and she arched into him as much as she was able.

At her movement, his teeth tugged on her nub while his lips formed a smile, but he didn't let go. Instead, he scraped his teeth back and forth across her hardened nipple. Moisture gathered between her folds. She swallowed a moan, not willing to end her sexual torture yet.

Sucking on her breast once again, he slowly lifted his mouth away, holding on to her until the last possible second. He looked up at her, one eyebrow raised.

She opened her mouth and licked her lips.

Wade's face froze as he stared at her mouth. His hands moved toward her face again, but then he shook his head. His finger pressed against her mouth. "I've already tasted these lips. It's time to taste your other lips."

Her eyes widened, her whole body tightening in anticipation.

"Good. Your expressions are more honest now."

She didn't dare say a word, not when his eyes promised her pleasure.

He knelt at her feet and his hands ducked under her skirt to clasp her calves. At his touch, she stiffened. When he ran his hands between the top of her short boots to her knees, she tensed at the frown on his face.

He glanced up. "Your left leg."

She wouldn't meet his gaze. "Just don't look at it."

"Kendra, look at me." His tone had softened.

Hesitantly, she brought her gaze back to his.

"Tell me."

She closed her eyes. Why hadn't she had it fixed? She certainly had the money now, but until this moment, she'd had other priorities.

"Kendra?"

Fine. He might as well know. Maybe then he'd leave her be and stop torturing her with his perfect self. "I was bit by a coyote when I was three. We lived in a trailer out in the Nevada desert. We had no money. My dad was who knows where, and we only had one car. Mom wrapped it up as best she could with strips from a sheet. When dad got home he said I didn't *need no doctor*. Three days later it was infected. My mother took me in the car while dad was passed out. We waited eight hours in the emergency room. When they finally saw me, they cut out all the rotten flesh in my calf and stitched me up. They said I should have skin grafts, but that kind of money was a pipedream."

Wade stood and brushed a tear from her cheek with his thumb. She hadn't thought about that time in her life since she started playing poker. She pulled herself together. "It's fine. I just cover it up. It's not a pretty sight."

Wade touched her forehead with his. "Of course it's fine. It's a part of you, who you are. I like who you are."

If she could move her arms, she'd hug him right now.

He pulled back and pressed a kiss on her forehead.

Okay, so now he would untie her and let her be.

When he knelt before her, a lump formed in her throat. She swallowed hard so she could speak. "You don't have to—."

"I want to." Wade's hands found her calves again, but this time he didn't hesitate. He stroked his hands upward. His thumbs tracing a path along her inner thighs, but not quite reaching her moist pussy. She wanted him to go there, lick her there.

His hands moved to her hips and his fingers hooked on to her panties and slowly brought them down to her boots. He patted her left leg. "Lift."

She did.

After he maneuvered the underwear over both her boots, he pushed one leg to the side, spreading her. He dropped her panties on a hay bale and even from where she stood tied, she could see a sheen on them.

He gazed up at her. "I'm going to taste you now. Remember, no noises."

Oh God. Just his words made her want to groan with need. He was expecting the impossible.

Wade lifted the hem of her jean skirt and ducked underneath it.

She squeaked in surprise.

He must not have heard because in the next instant his breath brushed her mound. His fingers combed through her curly hair before he explored her folds. First the outside lips, then the inside. One digit followed the path of moisture to her opening.

She held her breath, her pussy swelling with anticipation.

Wade's other arm snaked around her leg and grabbed her ass. She gasped silently at his large hand holding her in place. His finger at her opening slowly pushed forward, spreading her wet pussy, slipping in easily.

She bit her lip to keep from uttering a word. Instead, she squeezed her sheath.

He paused before pulling his hand back and adding another digit to invade her pussy. A few more times he pistoned inside her, the satisfaction of finally being speared drifting away as friction built.

Wade's tongue darted out and licked her clit. She bucked at the sudden stimulation and his hand on her ass steadied her. She closed her eyes as another swipe of his tongue had her tightening around his fingers again. Then with his hand on her ass, he pressed her mound toward his mouth and sucked her clit.

She gasped, grabbing the rope above her hands. Excitement burst through her core and spread outward. Her head felt light as every part of her focused on Wade's masterful mouth. His fingers, which had slowed, moved faster now, pumping her. She whimpered deep in her throat as waves of pleasure built upon each other. They stole her breath as her pussy tensed, finally sending her over the edge.

She thrust her head back and clenched her teeth as her scream erupted, unable to keep quiet any longer. Her back arched as her greedy clit conducted sweet fulfillment to her core.

Wade gave her clit a final kiss that had her jerking as his tongue connected with her sensitive flesh. His hand left her ass and he unhooked her leg from over his shoulder. She didn't remember moving it. As her weight settled on her feet, her hands started to tingle.

Wade ducked out from beneath her skirt and grinned up at her.

She stared at him a moment before she allowed herself to smile, her brain triggering her facial expressions faster now. "That was wonderful."

"So you liked your first lesson?"

She gave him a seductive look she hadn't used in years. It felt good. "Oh yes. Are there more?"

His grin turned predatory. "Definitely." He stilled. "Someone's here."

Her blood cooled instantly.

Wade stood and with a deft hand, he pulled a piece of the rope freeing her hands. How the hell did he do that?

In a moment, he'd jumped the rope off the peg and dropped it behind a hay bale. Grabbing his hat, he winked. "I'll keep them busy while you dress."

Pulling her bra together, she was once again pleased to have tried the front clasp, although she never expected it to be so useful in the ways it had already. Hearing voices outside, she quickly buttoned her shirt and tucked it in. She grabbed her new hat from the floor and dusted it off, ready to leave. A flash of white caught her eye. Pivoting, she sucked in her breath. Her lace panties lay half on top and half over the side of the hay bale.

The voices and the sound of crunching gravel came closer. Snatching up her underwear, she stuffed it inside her left boot, and moved toward the entryway.

As Wade and Lacey entered, she was petting one of the gray riding horses. Wade hadn't told her their names yet. She'd have him order name plates for their stalls. She'd bet her new boots her customers would love knowing their mount's name.

"Kendra." Wade's voice was far too serious and she moved around the horse to meet them.

Lacey looked about to cry.

"Tell me."

"Our electricity is gone. All of it."

Kendra touched Lacey's arm. "I'm sure there's electricity somewhere in Arizona. Let's see if we can't figure out where we fit in that picture. Okay?" She gave the young woman a kind smile.

Lacey sniffed and straightened her shoulders. "Right. From what I could tell, all of the resort is without power. I was just coming here to see if Wade had any electricity on this end."

"Wade, can you throw on the stable lights?"

He strode to the switch bank and threw each one. "Nothing. Let me check the office just to be thorough."

Once Wade had left, Kendra turned to Lacey. "How long has it been out?"

"Not long. Selma was in the kitchen making Tres Leches cake for tonight's dessert. She yelled and Adriana ran in. When they couldn't find any fuses blown, they called me. I haven't found Billy yet. I thought we should check the garage too."

"Good idea." She started for her golf cart. "The other side of the canyon receives electricity directly from the dirt road. If we can isolate where the problem is, we can get it fixed. Let's go."

Lacey hopped in. "I know we have a generator, but I wasn't sure if Billy ever bought the gas for it."

"Yes, he did. The good news is it will keep all our refrigeration units going as well as the air conditioning in the main building.

The bad news is, that is all it can handle." She drove the cart over to Wade's office.

He was exiting the building. "No electricity in there either. I'll grab my cart and come over."

"Thanks."

As she headed down the path, she glanced back toward the barn. Wade was already getting in his cart, but there was another there as well. She shook her head. Billy.

"What's wrong?"

She glanced at Lacey, her concern crinkling her pretty forehead. "Nothing. I just figured out where Billy is."

"Oh."

Lacey didn't ask where because they were all aware of Billy's problem. He was doing better, but barely.

As they pulled up to the main building, Adriana and Selma stepped out. Kendra's heart swelled. Every one of them was concerned. Her dream had become theirs. She stopped the cart and walked toward them, ready to assure them when Adriana pointed. "Look."

Turning, she looked across the canyon. Blue light flashed like a warning beacon, probably amplified by the metal side of the garage. "Ah hell, what now?"

Wade drove up. "I'll go get him. I can check the electricity while I'm over there."

"Him?"

He raised an eyebrow. "Of course. It has to be Harper."

"Right. Thanks."

She turned back toward the women. "I guess we wait. In the meantime, let's get the generator running. Adriana, can you help me with that?"

"Sure."

"Lacey, why don't you and Selma bring us a tray of iced teas and sodas? I don't want us drinking anything stronger until the sheriff leaves."

"Good idea."

Kendra headed toward the end of the great room with Adriana. When they reached the back hallway, they entered the small utility room, which had no windows. Damn, what had she'd been thinking when she designed that?

Adriana pulled out her cell phone and switched it to flashlight. She shrugged. "The service may be spotty out here, but the battery lasts a long time."

Kendra grinned, finding it easier to fall into the habit of revealing her emotions now that she'd started. And boy, had she started. How was she going to stop having sex with Wade when she couldn't resist him?

"Do you know what to do?"

"No…I mean yes." Rerouting her brain from Wade to the electricity took a bit of effort, but she managed. She threw the switch to take the main building off the grid and pushed the button for the generator. They could hear it roar to life outside at the back of the building.

Adriana flicked the room's light switch. "Oh no. It didn't work. Now what?"

Kendra moved the master switch one more notch. "Try the light now."

The room was blasted with white florescent light.

"Woo hoo! You did it."

She grinned. "We did it." She'd done everything she'd set out to do with a whole lot of help from her friends, and in less than two days, her dream would come true. Would Buddy and Ginger ever find this place? She hoped so.

Pride and confidence had her closing the utility room door with a thud. She would have to do something special to thank everyone. She couldn't have done it without them. "Let's go. I want to find out why Harper is here. He's never come with flashing lights before, unless Wade's wrong and it's someone else."

Adriana put her hands on her hips. "I hope he isn't here on official business, like to shut us down for something we were unaware of. Or maybe Wade was wrong and the bird's nest was a bald eagle's."

A chill ran up Kendra's spine at Adriana's words. To have come so close and be cut off at the pass would be too much to accept. Turning the corner, she found Lacey and Selma sitting in the main foyer sipping on sodas and watching the progress of the cart coming up the path, Harper's distinctive uniform too obvious to ignore.

Searching for a calm she didn't feel, Kendra grabbed an iced tea and leaned against the front desk, unwilling to show any of the turmoil in her heart, especially to the sheriff. So much for leaving her poker face behind.

Harper entered first, followed by Wade. She glanced at her stableman but he shrugged. Harper must have been close-lipped about his reason for being here. It wasn't as if the two were best buddies.

She moved away from the counter. "Hello, Sheriff. I'm afraid we are out of electricity, but I can offer you a cold soda or iced tea."

Harper took off his hat and wiped his brow. "It feels pretty cool in here. Do you have a generator?"

"Yes, we do." She'd been about to tell him the limitations of her generator, but changed her mind. She was more interested in why his blue lights were flashing.

"That's good, real good." Despite his words, he seemed disappointed, even uncomfortable. "Wow, you look very nice today. Is it a special occasion?"

"No." She didn't like the way he eyed her. "Was there something you came by for, or were you just checking in on us?"

His face grew stern and her heart beat double-time.

"Actually, I'm here about your lack of electricity. Thought you should know some joy riding twentysomethings were four-wheeling in their pickup truck and they slammed into one of the telephone poles that brings electricity down your road. The damn thing must have been pretty old, because it cracked and came down."

Wade stepped up. "Is everyone all right? I didn't see any red ambulance lights when I was over at the garage."

Harper turned. "No, you wouldn't. The responsible persons have already been transported and the vehicle towed."

Kendra studied the sheriff. "Wow, that was fast. We just lost electricity a half hour ago."

"Yeah. The pole didn't fall completely until the truck was pulled away from it. That's when you probably lost power. We didn't realize it would fall. Scared the livin' shit out of us, if you'll excuse the language."

"I bet." Wade, usually so easy to read, was hiding his thoughts, and it bugged her.

Harper moved forward. "If you don't mind, I could use one of those sodas."

She gestured toward the front desk where the cans sat in a bowl of ice. "Help yourself. I imagine overseeing an accident like that is thirsty work."

He nodded, and she looked at Wade once Harper passed her. Wade shook his head. What was he thinking?

She turned to face the sheriff, who was guzzling down a ginger ale. "Thank you for letting us know. I guess we'll just have to wait until the electric company fixes the pole."

Harper set his empty can on the counter and picked up an iced tea. "May I?"

"Of course."

He moved closer to her. "You may want to delay your opening. A single business is never a first priority for the electric company and this is a major project, installing a new pole. If they get out here in the next four weeks, I'd be impressed."

"Four weeks?" She couldn't wait four weeks. She had people coming in two days and she'd be damned if she would delay opening.

Harper put his hand on her shoulder. "I'm sorry. It seems such a shame good people have to suffer because of reckless ones. Maybe this is a sign for you to relax. Maybe take a couple weeks off and then come back with new perspective."

Perspective? What the hell was wrong with her perspective? Kendra resisted the urge to smack the man's hand off her shoulder and instead moved away abruptly. "We appreciate your kindness, Sheriff. Now, as you can imagine, I have a lot of arrangements to make. Lacey, please take the sheriff back to his car."

"I will leave you to your planning." Harper tipped his hat. "Have a good evening."

As soon as the man left, Adriana leapt up. "That man doesn't want you to open."

Selma stood up a bit slower, but was just as quick to voice her opinion. "I agree. That sheriff is a prick. He doesn't want you running this place. He wants his women in bed and the kitchen only."

Kendra raised her brows at that. "Lucky for me, he has no say in the matter. Adriana, did you put the champagne in the four casitas already?"

"Yeah. Oh, hell. I'll go take those bottles out and bring them back here before we lose daylight."

Selma shuffled past them. "I need to put my damn cake in the oven and start on dinner. At least my kitchen works."

When the women left, she turned to Wade. "You don't believe him."

"No, I don't."

"Why?"

"Just a hunch. I'm going to give it fifteen minutes then I'm taking Buca for a ride. I'll be back by sunset."

She frowned, easily falling into revealing her feelings with him. "Why not take a golf cart and your truck?"

"Let's just say, I want to have an excuse and riding a new horse around to see how she handles is the perfect one."

"Do you think Harper is dangerous?"

Wade looked toward the windows facing the canyon. "I don't know, but I plan to find out."

She grasped his hand. "I don't want you to put yourself in danger. This is my resort. I should do it."

He pulled her closer and gazed into her eyes. His lips curved up just a fraction. "First, you don't even know how to ride. Second, in case you hadn't noticed, this isn't just your resort."

She opened her mouth to argue, but he placed his finger across her lips. "Un-uh, your resort is going to open because everyone you saw here tonight loves it and wants it to succeed as much as you do."

At the truth in his words, warmth radiated out from her heart, through her body and all the way down to her toes. "Even you?"

He cupped the side of her neck and brushed his thumb along her jaw. "Especially me." Lowering his face, he kissed her. The kiss held so much promise she wanted to cry from the possibilities, and her heart opened wide.

As he pulled back, he stared at her like he wanted to say more, but then his expression turned serious. "As much as I would prefer to kiss you for the next fifteen minutes, I think we need to talk about who is behind this sabotage to your property."

"Yes." She pushed away the contentment of being in his arms to focus on the most pressing matter. "You think someone is causing these problems too?"

"Yes. First Game and Fish hearing about the nest and now this."

She flopped down in a lobby chair. "That's not the half of it. The beer cooler cord was cut, I've had a hand-sink drain clogged when no one but Selma uses it, as well as cracked windows and pulled-out watering lines. But everyone who was here just now is absolutely loyal to me."

He raised his brows and stared at her. "I didn't know you had more issues." He moved to the front desk and grabbed an iced tea.

Popping the top, he swallowed a couple mouthfuls, just enough for her to be distracted by his Adam's apple moving within his corded neck.

He wiped his mouth on his sleeve and continued. "So if everyone on your staff who was here just now is loyal, that leaves Billy, Powell, and the sheriff."

CHAPTER EIGHT

Billy, Powell and Harper. Of the three, Kendra wanted it to be Harper. "I can't believe it could be Billy. He—" How much had Wade discerned about her landscaper?

Wade studied her. "You know Billy is a drunk."

She couldn't meet his gaze. What must he, the perfect man, think about her having an employee like Billy? "Yes, I know." She straightened her stance, not willing to be judged on her hiring practices. "But Billy never fails me and he's improving. I know his weakness and so does he."

"Is that why he's so loyal to you? You are the only one who will give an old drunk a job?"

She shifted her weight to her right hip. "You make it sound like I'm manipulating him. I'm not. I just offered him the job. He didn't have to take it."

Wade raised an eyebrow. "Where did you meet Billy?"

She relaxed, unaware until that moment that Wade's opinion meant so much to her. Something to ponder. "I met him in Key West while at a tournament. He was homeless only because he spent his social security on booze, but he was such a sweet man, I remembered him and looked for him every time I was down there." She smiled sadly at the memory. "He started sobering up when the tournament came to town just so we could go out and get a bite to eat. He even treated me once, which I know meant he wouldn't have as much to drink that month."

"I think he worships the very ground you walk on."

"What?" She stared at him, startled.

Wade shook his head. "Don't be so surprised. You've done a lot for him. Besides, he's the one who dragged me away from my work when Game and Fish arrived. He's loyal to the core."

She turned away, not wanting him to see how teary-eyed she'd become thinking of Billy. He was such a kind soul. He just needed someone to look out for him.

"That narrows it down to Powell and Harper." Wade's voice had lowered and she turned to look at him.

"I can't believe it's Powell. He would have gone to jail if I hadn't offered him a job."

Wade grinned. "So you only hire people who are in need of work? I can't wait to find out about Adriana, Selma and Lacey." He held up his hand as she was about to speak. "But we have more pressing matters. First, satisfy my curiosity about Powell. What was his crime?"

She shrugged. "He was a hacker. He'd hacked into my personal checking account, which is how I met him. I was supposed to testify against him, but after talking with him I offered him a choice, come work for me and I'd drop the charges, or go to jail."

Wade broke into laughter and she couldn't help grinning. When she viewed her staff from his perspective, it truly was the motley crew she privately dubbed them. "So that leaves Harper."

Wade sobered instantly. "It does. He definitely knew about the bird's nest and was somehow involved in this electricity issue. But he hasn't been the one clogging drains, ripping up watering lines and causing all the problems around here. Someone would have seen him. He'd have to drive his car out here and have some pretty strong motivation to do so. Has he ever said you shouldn't open a nudist resort? I doubt that sits well with people in this area."

"No. I think, as Selma pointed out, he has more of an issue with me being the boss than anything else."

Wade stared out the resort's floor-to-ceiling windows. "What about the torn-up watering lines for the plants? Did you see any footsteps around those areas?"

"No. It was pretty scratched up like an animal." She sighed. Some of these occurrences could very well be due to natural causes, like a casita settling and cracking a window and some may be a particular person adding to the problems, like informing Game and Fish about a nest. "I'm betting on Harper."

Wade turned and smirked. "Don't go all-in on that bet yet."

She laughed and gave him a wink. "I promise not to if you promise not to fold before the final hand."

Wade froze at Kendra's full-throated laugh. This side of her was new and intoxicating. His body tensed with wanting and he wished he could explore it more, but with the sun soon to set, he needed to investigate the "crash" site. "One way to get the full story on this power outage is to ride up to the road. I'll head out now so I can be back in time for Selma's quesadillas."

Kendra shook her head. "You even know what's for dinner tonight? Hmmm, if I didn't know better, I'd say she was sweet on you."

He loved this teasing side of her. If only it would last. He shrugged. "Maybe I'm just a bit sweet on her."

Kendra's smile was warm and relaxed. "I'll be sure to let her know. Now go see what you can find out. I have a resort with no electricity to get ready for guests."

"Yes, Ms. Lowe."

She gave him a scowl, but couldn't hold it long, especially when he pulled her close and gave her a stirring goodbye kiss. At least he hoped it stirred her blood because it certainly did his. Letting her go, he turned and strode out the door with a strange urge to whistle.

By the time he returned to his office, he was very sure whoever was causing the problems for Kendra also had something to do with the managers leaving. He sent off a quick email to Dale to let him know his latest suspicions before heading out to the barn.

After saddling Buca, he mounted and guided her down the dirt road. Once he topped the other side of the canyon, he could see the broken telephone pole. From where he sat, it looked like a turkey vulture stooped over to eat its meal of carrion. An eerie sight, but what concerned him more was the massive brown wall of dust in the distance. If he turned back, all tracks would be gone before he could return. He'd have to make this quick. Riding closer, the image of the pole grew larger and the outline of splintered wood came into view.

Wade pulled up Buca and jumped down, tying the mare's reins to a mesquite tree. He carefully walked around the site, which still had power lines on the ground. He wasn't taking any chances. Some of them could be live.

From the tire tracks in the road, there had been only one vehicle. He crouched and examined the ground. There was only one type of footprint as well. He would have lost that bet. How did one man crash a vehicle into a pole, break it and drive away?

He attempted to move closer to examine the pole, but the wires were too much of a hazard and his time was limited. He jogged back to Buca and gave her a pat. "I don't know, girl. Something isn't right here."

Mounting, he looked back toward the pole and a shiver raced up his spine. The wall of dust was now less than a mile away. This haboob had traveled fast and was headed directly for the resort. "Shit."

Kicking Buca into a gallop, he made for the garage. What had he been thinking? He'd grown up with these monster sandstorms. He had to get Buca under cover. Racing down the dirt road, he felt the telltale grit buffet his back.

Just a few yards more.

As soon as they reached the three-walled shelter, he rode Buca inside and brought her up behind his truck. Quickly, he tied her to the bumper and opened the tail gate. He retrieved an old blanket from the metal box mounted in the bed. Dust and stones banged against the garage's three metal sides. Hopefully, it was built according to code or he and Buca would be buried. Confidence in Kendra's quality control took that worry away.

Draping the blanket over his horse, he lay down in the bed of the truck. The noise increased as the powerful winds picked up dirt, rocks, plants, everything from the desert floor, and whipped them into a frenzy. Loud pings hit the truck. Staying low in the bed, he kept an eye on Buca.

"It's okay, girl. Just keep your head down. It'll be over in no time."

The horse moved from side to side as sticks and sand hit her. Luckily, the speed of those items was nothing inside the garage when compared to outside. Still, they could cut. The dust beneath the shelter became thicker and Wade covered his mouth with his shirt. Still he soothed the horse.

"It's almost over. I'll be sure to bring you an apple for putting up with my stupidity."

A loud thump drew his attention and Buca neighed, very unhappy with her situation.

"I'm sorry, girl. This is my fault. I should have turned back." He checked the reins to be sure they were secure to the truck, but still a horse could snap them if truly afraid. Buca, however, was a well-trained horse and from the valley. She had to have experienced haboobs before.

Another loud thump against the wall of the garage had the horse pulling on her reins again and Wade lifted his head to see if the storm lessened at all. He had his head above the truck bed for no more than a few seconds, just enough to see if it was lighter outside, when a rock caught him above his right eye. He ducked down again. "Shit. Now I'm a certified idiot." Taking his shirt from around his mouth, he wiped at the blood dripping down his face.

Instead of being smart and returning to the resort, he'd been too bent on helping Kendra and finding proof that the sheriff had caused the electrical outage, which it was clear he did, although how he did it was still a mystery. The real question was why? Why was Harper so bent on Kendra not opening? Was it because she was the boss or because it was a nudist resort?

Wade couldn't blame Harper for not wanting the resort to open. Wade wasn't excited about it either, or rather about working around naked people, but he'd at least tell her outright. He flushed. No, he wouldn't. He hadn't. Shit. He'd told her everyone wanted her dream to succeed, but in actuality, he wanted her dream to succeed but the naked part of the resort to fail. What did that make him?

A hypocrite. But at least he wasn't sabotaging her. Still, it didn't set well with him that he hadn't told her how he felt. Why did it have to be a nudist resort? She could simply make it a resort. The more important question was, why was he concerned about telling her how he felt?

The answer came as quickly as the question. He liked her. A lot. There was strength in her and yet he'd found the soft spots underneath. Truth be told, he was attracted to all her parts. He grinned, the memory of being between her legs in the barn caused his dick to grow hard. Yup, he liked everything about her. Maybe even more than "like."

No, he wasn't going down that path until he fulfilled his obligation to Dale and helped Kendra stop the sabotage. He never wanted her to know the real reason he'd come to Poker Flat. His gut assured him it would not set well with her even if it was to her benefit.

Buca whinnied, interrupting his musings. Wade listened to the slowing noises against the metal walls. It should be safe enough to look above the bed of the truck again. A red hue glowed outside, although there was still some swirling sand particles in the air. Deeming it safe enough to check on his horse, he climbed out of the truck and removed the blanket from Buca.

He ran his hands down her coat. "I think you weathered that storm better than I did." She nuzzled her face against his shoulder. "You are definitely a keeper." He smiled. Maybe Kendra was too. Brushing the mare's coat as best he could with his hands, he finally mounted her and headed outside. The sky was darkening, the red hue having given way to purples and pinks. It must be about a half hour after sunset. Guess he missed dinner.

He shrugged as he guided the horse down the canyon path, thankful she hadn't been hurt. Missing dinner was a small price for him to pay for finding the truth. He'd feed Buca her dinner right away, get her combed and bedded for the night, then see what he could find in the kitchen for himself.

~~~~~~

Kendra glanced at the clock for the umpteenth time. It was 9:17p.m. The sun had set two hours ago. Where was he? She couldn't concentrate because Wade hadn't been seen yet. Billy drove over to the stables after the haboob rolled out, but Wade and Buca weren't there. Was he all right?

She'd called over to his office, but the phone lines were down too. She really needed to find a booster or something for the cell coverage. Once the sandstorm hit, the reception was nil so that option was out. "Where are you, Wade?" Maybe she should go look.

A knock on the door was a welcome distraction. "Come in."

"Hey, boss, do you have a minute?"

"Of course, Powell. What is it?"

The young man strode forward, taking off his baseball cap with security printed across the crown. Something he had asked be part of his uniform. "I need to tell you something."

Kendra tensed. Did he find another problem? She couldn't find it in her to smile, but she tried to sound relaxed. "Please do. I always want to hear what my employees have to say."

He looked away. "I don't want you to be mad at me. I didn't hack into anything, I promise."

He was well aware to do so would mean his immediate dismissal. She didn't doubt him for a moment. "Powell, what did you do?"

The man turned his hat in his hands, his nervousness obvious. "I may have read someone's emails, but the computer was on and the person nowhere to be found. I couldn't resist, but then I saw what was written and knew I had to tell you."

He must have stumbled upon her saboteur. Kendra braced herself to be hurt by one of her own people. "Tell me what?"

He finally looked at her. "Wade Johnson has been writing to someone named Dale. I think he may be reporting on you and the resort. He mentioned a lot of details about the issues we have here."

Her heart lurched at the information and slowly shriveled. She wanted to be sick. What the hell was Wade doing telling Dale what went on here? Why spy on her unless it was to kill her operation? Was Wade the saboteur and trying to throw suspicion on others? Her body heated with the betrayal, but she wouldn't let Powell know that. "Exactly what did he write?"

Powell looked away again. "I'm not sure. I don't have a good memory and I didn't completely understand it, but it didn't sound good."

Seated behind her desk, she gripped the arms of her chair. "Thank you for letting me know, but don't ever look at someone else's computer again unless I ask you to. That is my prerogative, not yours. I don't want other employees distrusting you. If they do, so will the guests, and I can't have that."

"Yes, boss."

"Was there anything else?" She sincerely hoped not because she barely held back her tears as it was.

"Nope. That's all. I'll get back to my rounds now." Powell donned his baseball cap.

She nodded, not trusting her voice.

After he shut the door, she let Wade's betrayal sink in and it cut across her heart with a fierceness that took her breath away. It echoed what her ex-husband had done to her, but with him, she'd always expected him to find someone better. Wade had made her believe in him. Hurt, anger, and questions spun like a microburst through her body. She stood, unable to sit still a moment longer.

Had he disappeared because of what he'd done? Wherever he was, she would find him. She wanted to know everything and she wanted to know *now*.

Grabbing a flashlight, she stalked out into the night air. The sound of a coyote in the distance made her shiver. She'd never overcome that particular fear. Jumping into her golf cart, she drove to Wade's casita on the off chance he'd come back and simply gone to bed. If he was asleep, she'd wake him.

Taking her ring of keys, she found the one to his door and opened it. The flashlight beam revealed the man was as neat in his home as in the barn. Striding to the bedroom, she pulled the door open, but even before the light of her flashlight hit the bed, she sensed no one was there. "Damn."

Worry wormed its way back into her heart, but she thrust it aside. She should go through his belongings, but she just couldn't bring herself to do so, at least not until she confronted him. She let herself out and locked the door. Next stop, the barn.

As she drove the short distance to the stables, she prayed she'd find him there. At least then she would know he wasn't hurt. What was she thinking? He'd hurt her, crushed her, and probably didn't even care. As she topped the hill, feeble light from the barn spread into the dirt parking area. Someone had one of their battery-operated lanterns. Was Powell making his rounds or was Wade back?

Stepping into the barn, she froze. Wade was naked, his back to her as he dried off his hair, his back rippling with his movements, his ass gleaming with water droplets. He must have used the outside shower. Despite her anger, her body responded to seeing so much male.

He turned around, his eyes widening at the sight of her. "Hey, what are you doing out here so late at night?"

Her gaze swept over him of its own accord. The wet hair on his chest emphasized the mounds of his pectoral muscles. She followed the wet line of hair that bisected his abs all the way to his cock. Swallowing, she forced herself to look at his face. A cut above his eye beaded with blood. Before she could stop, she took a step forward. Catching herself, she halted and pointed to his eye. "What happened?"

"I was stupid, that's what happened." He shook his head as he wiped down his chest, obviously in no hurry to cover himself. "I underestimated how fast the haboob was moving and Buca and I had to take shelter in the garage. I just finished brushing the sand off her coat. I'm glad I was the one cut and not her."

"Do you need stitches?"

He patted the towel above his eye and looked at the blood staining it. "Shit. It started again. The shower must have reopened it. Nothing a Band-Aid can't fix." His grin was crooked, making it hard to stay mad.

But she wasn't simply mad. The anger was intertwined with a pain far too close to her heart and the damnable question of why. Fisting her hands, she took another step closer. "What are you hiding from me? What are you telling Dale? Why are you really here, Wade?"

His grin faded. "Who told you?"

At his admission, her stomach tightened so hard she almost doubled over, but she'd be damned if she'd show him how much he hurt her. "It doesn't matter. I want to hear it from you. The truth, that is." She kept her poker face firmly in place. He didn't deserve to know how she felt.

Wade wrapped the towel around his hips and strode toward her. "I had hoped if I figured it out, you'd never need to know. I didn't want to hurt you."

"Figured out what?"

He stopped a couple feet away from her. Maybe he sensed she wasn't exactly happy with him at the moment.

"Why your other stable managers quit. Dale asked me to look into it. He can't afford to have a problem with his staffing placements and he wanted to know why well-qualified men left this job early. It doesn't reflect well on his new company."

That wasn't what she'd expected. She took a step back. "Did you discover anything?"

"From what I've pieced together, none of them were unhappy. I think they may have been blackmailed into quitting."

She raised her brow, unable to hide her surprise. "Blackmailed? With what?"

"I'm not sure. I think the last one was into pornography and he was threatened with having that revealed to you." He gave her a smirk. "These men Dale found wouldn't be aware of your penchant for hiring misfits. So if Michael thought you would fire him, my guess is he would quit first." His smile turned sheepish. "Men are like that."

Her heart responded to his look even as she held on to her hurt. He'd still betrayed her. "So how did someone know Michael liked pornography? How did you know?"

Wade took another step closer. "If Harper wanted you to close, he could have done some investigating. I discovered it when I was going through the files on the office computer."

Her heart sped at how close they were to finding the person responsible for so many of her troubles. "Let me see them."

"I deleted them. They were inappropriate, especially on a business computer. I also didn't want you to think I had downloaded them. As the boss, you can search through anyone's computer."

Deleted? That was convenient. She tried to read him like she did her opponents at the poker table. The problem was, in this case, she wanted to believe him. Her objectivity with this man disappeared down a rattlesnake hole the day she met him. Besides, she'd known Michael had liked pornography from Adriana, but the woman wouldn't have told anyone. Still, he'd known if he was caught with it he would be fired on the spot.

Wade was right. She could search through anyone's computer, but employees weren't supposed to and Powell had. "Wade, when did you get back to the barn?"

His brows lowered at the sudden change in topic. "About an hour after sunset. So maybe eight-thirty. Why?"

"Get dressed and meet me in your office. I think I know who our saboteur might be."

He grinned. "That's the first time a woman has asked me to put my clothes *on*."

"Ugh." She rolled her eyes and stalked out of the barn. Some men's egos were just too much. The last thing she wanted him to know was that without his clothes he was too much of a distraction to her thought process.

Walking into his dark office, the red glow of the exit sign her only light, she hit her hip on his desk. "Damn." Now how the hell had Powell found the emails if there was no electricity?

The answer was clear. He didn't find them tonight. He came in earlier in the day when he should have been sleeping or he knew about them days earlier. Either way, she now had to put him back on her suspect list.

Wasting no time, she turned on the battery back-up below the desk. It wouldn't last long, so she sat and zipped through Wade's emails. After reading three sent to Dale Osborn, her stomach loosened up. Wade had told the truth. She wasn't happy with Dale or with Wade's secrecy, but as a business person, she understood it. She'd have to think seriously about whether or not to use Dale's company again.

If Powell had read these same emails, he would know they didn't implicate Wade in the sabotage of the resort, but he had cast doubt on Wade's character anyway. That didn't make Powell responsible for all that had gone wrong, necessarily. He could have simply been protecting her. She really didn't want it to be Powell.

Wade walked in and placed his hat on the file cabinet. "You didn't believe me." His scowl in the glow of the computer's light made it clear he was upset.

"Actually, I did. What I wanted to see was what you had written to make Powell doubt you."

Wade sat on the corner of his desk. "Powell? You think he might be behind your troubles? But didn't you say he was loyal?"

She pondered that. Powell telling her Wade was spying on her was the act of someone who was loyal. "I think he is. I'm just not sure. He's the one who went into your computer and read these emails. Either he suspected you of being the culprit, or he is and he wants me to fire you. I just don't know which."

Wade looked over her head, his gaze clearly somewhere other than the dark room. Then his lips formed a slow grin. She'd seen that same grin on his face earlier that afternoon, in the barn.

"I have an idea on how we can flush out our culprit."

"How?"

He shook his head and stood. "I have to see more curiosity than that."

Huh, oh. She tilted her head and squinted up at him. "How?"

He chuckled. "That's better. If this person, be it Powell or Harper or someone we don't suspect at all has blackmailed all the former stable managers, maybe we can get him or her to blackmail me."

She rolled her eyes. "Again, how?"

"Promote me."

"Promote you? To what?"

He came around the desk, his energy fueling her own. "I don't know. Something that sounds important. If this person thinks you'll depend on me, need me, then that might just force his hand."

Her shoulders slumped. "Yeah, but for that to work, you'd have to be easily blackmailed, meaning you'd have to have a vice. Unfortunately for us, you're perfect."

Wade's laughter caught her off guard.

"What? Are you laughing at me?"

He shook his head as he attempted to contain his amusement. "No, no. I've just never had anyone think me perfect before. I need you to have a chat with my mom. You might even want to ask Dale or even Buca how perfect I am. Trust me, you'll get a totally different perspective."

"It's not that funny." She pouted, the expression coming naturally. "As you have pointed out, I've hired a group of outcasts from 'normal' society. Compared to them, you are, well…boring."

He stared at her in shock, and she couldn't help the giggle that surfaced.

"Boring? I'll show you boring." He pulled her out of his chair and threw her over his shoulder.

"Wade! Wade, what are you doing?"

He didn't answer. Striding through the building in the pitch black as if he knew it like the back of his hand, he stalked down the back hall. At the end, he opened the door to the metal barn she'd hoped to host parties in, if she ever figured out what to do with the reproduction stagecoach she'd won in a game down in Tombstone.

The large area appeared bright with its emergency lights compared to the darkness of the rest of the building. Wade strode to the stagecoach. Without hesitating, he opened the door and dumped her inside.

"Hey."

"I'll show you boring." The tone of his voice caused ripples of anticipation to spike through her.

Climbing in after her, he shut the door and sat on one of the seats. He pulled her up and positioned her between his legs. "Kneel."

His face was tense, revealing nothing, but when she glanced at his jeans, a large bulge was clear, and she licked her lips. Kneeling, she immediately unzipped him and nudged his jeans down his hips, but before she could touch him, he stopped her.

"Uh-huh. I don't want your mouth, I want your breasts."

Her pussy swelled at his words and she willingly unbuttoned her shirt. Happy for the second time that day that she had on her new front-clasp bra, she quickly popped it open and shrugged out of it. Naked from the waist up, she released the clip that held her hair, knowing how much he liked it down. His intake of breath made her grin, pleased she could excite him with such a simple move.

She leaned forward, pulling his hard cock toward her then used her hands on her breasts to sandwich his long, thick dick.

"Yesss."

She glanced up to see Wade's eyes closed and her own need took a backseat to pleasuring him.

Slowly, she moved her breasts up and down, squeezing his cock between them. His breathing increased and pre-cum leaked from the small hole at the tip. She stopped moving and licked it off while still keeping him captive. The head was just too close to resist. Lowering her face, she took the tip into her mouth.

His moan was followed by his hand burying itself in her hair, encouraging her in her attentions. She scraped her teeth around the ridge and lightly tugged on it before nibbling across the tip.

"Kendra, you are too good at that."

His hands drew hers away from her breasts and he gripped her shoulders, pulling her up.

She tried to twist away. "I want to feel you come in my mouth."

"Not now. I need to be inside you too much."

She had no warning. One minute she was standing half naked and the next he had tugged down her skirt, leaving her in only her boots.

He grasped her hips, his thumbs rubbing her sides. "Hey, where are those pretty lace panties you were wearing earlier?"

She glanced at her left boot. "I didn't have time to put them on when Lacey arrived at the barn." She shrugged. "I guess I forgot about them."

"I think you should forget about them more often." He wiggled his brows and she laughed.

He was so easy to be with. He made her want to be with him all the time. She watched as he pulled a condom from the front pocket of his jeans and tore it open. He unrolled it down his length, her pussy contracting with excitement.

"Come here."

She didn't need to be asked twice. Settling her knees on either side of him, she positioned her opening over his head, barely touching it. Unable to resist, she stroked herself against his cock, back and forth from her opening to her clit, her nipples brushing across his denim shirt.

"Fuck, woman. You're killing me."

Grinning at her perfect cowboy's language, she stopped teasing. Grasping his hard shoulders, she slowly lowered herself on him. He was large and every inch of the sheathing was excruciating pleasure. When she was fully impaled, she gazed into his eyes.

There was no smile or scowl, just a sense of wonder.

She felt it too. A sense of perfect. *I love you.*

CHAPTER NINE

The words crept up Kendra's throat, but she swallowed them down. The feeling too new to share, a wild card she wasn't accustomed to playing with.

Wade's arms wrapped around her like steel bands and he kissed her, his tongue plunging into her mouth like his cock between her legs.

When his pelvis pressed up, she sucked hard on his tongue. She couldn't get close enough. She clasped his head to her and rocked against him. He matched her movements, adding friction against her clit as he pushed into her.

Her body flowed against him as he stroked her need tighter. Tension built in her core and she pulled her mouth away, needing air to gasp as the sensations whipped through her.

Wade's mouth found her right breast and sucked, his tongue stroking her nipple. His arms loosened, allowing her to arch back as he grasped her ass. He kneaded her there, but kept them glued together.

Her blood flowed to her pussy, thickening the tight passage around his cock as it pushed in and out. She arched farther and his arm came around to support her, the friction between her thighs keeping her on the edge.

Then his finger stroked her clit and her world ignited. She yelled out her pleasure as her sheath convulsed around him. His shout barely penetrated her consciousness, but the heat of his cum exploded within her like gasoline added to a raging fire. She screamed as the inferno engulfed them, taking them together in an exquisite blaze.

As she floated back to earth like a piece of ash, Wade pulled her up and hugged her tight, his breathing as rough as hers. For the first time in her life, she felt cherished, taken care of. It was a tempting place to be.

Wade held Kendra in his arms, loving the feel of her relaxed against him. He was hooked on her, from enjoying her passion, to her stoic strength, to her insecurity about revealing a perceived deformity. All these facets and more drew him closer to her, like he'd been hypnotized by an Arizona peridot.

Was he being naïve again like he'd been in college? She'd obviously had a full life so far. One he couldn't imagine living, nor did he want to, but having her in his arms made him want to stay with her. He could almost hear Dale now, telling him he was a fool.

Ignoring that voice of reason, he kissed her hair, inhaling the flowery-nut scent that caused his cock to stir to life again. His brain and his heart could argue all day if he let them, but his cock was absolutely sure about her.

She lifted her head, eyes wide. "You want more?"

He raised an eyebrow and smirked. "Yes. That is one of my many flaws. I can't get enough of you."

Her chest rose with her intake of breath, but it was the squeezing of her sheath that had him moving. Grasping her hips, he hauled her off him.

"Oh." Her disappointment stoked his ego, but the cool air after being inside her was harsh against his dick. Pulling a bandana out of his back pocket, he wrapped the used condom and put it aside. He produced another one and waved it in front of her. "I'll just put this here because we're going to need it."

She stepped between his legs again. "Good, I'm already cooling off."

"We can't have that." Grasping her waist, he lifted his face to nuzzle beneath her left breast. Playfully, he licked his way to her areola and finally took the taught nipple between his teeth. Lightly, he nibbled.

She jerked away. "You make me hot too fast."

"There's no such thing as too fast. Now take off your boots."

He sensed the second she tensed.

"Because there won't be room for your boots." He wiggled his brows to help her relax.

Reluctantly, she did as requested. In the glow of the garage's emergency lights that shone through the stagecoach windows, he viewed the damage done to her calf. A third of it was gone, but the tissue was well scarred over from the intervening years. Still, he could understand why a woman would be self-conscious. He'd bet high school in particular had been hard for her.

She stood, leaning on her right hip. Aha. That stance was her "tell." It signaled she was uncomfortable for one reason or another. It wouldn't be obvious while sitting at a poker table. No wonder she'd been so successful. The question was, why was she uncomfortable now?

"I'm not so sure I like you being in charge."

He grinned. So the lady enjoyed being the boss. "I think it only fair I have a turn."

"What do you mean? You just—"

"No, *you* controlled our pleasure and I have to admit, you are excellent at it."

The blush that rose to her cheeks reminded him of the perfect color of her pussy folds. He gestured to the floor with his hand in invitation. "If you would be willing to get on your hands and knees, I can try to match your skill."

She sighed. "If you insist."

He couldn't see her face, but he sensed her willingness. She was playing once again. He loved that she was comfortable with him when they made love. He learned more about her during sex than any other time.

As she knelt, he yanked off his boots then stood as best he could in the confines of the coach and dropped his jeans and underwear to the floor.

He'd only reached the second button of his shirt when she presented him with her ass. His cock jumped to attention at the offering, and he pulled his shirt over his head. Kneeling behind her, he stroked his hand down her spine to the base of her crease. Her body remained still, but he could smell her anticipation. Lightly, he continued his travel with two fingers, barely spreading her cheeks. When he reached her pussy, he stopped, made her wait, building her need.

His own body responded as well and he wouldn't be able to tease for much longer, but he wanted her ready for him. His stomach tensed with concern. This position would put him deeper, and with her small size, he wanted to be sure she was loose enough. He wouldn't hurt her, no matter how much he wanted this.

"Wade, don't stop." Her breathy voice made his cock harden further in anticipation.

"Very well. If you insist." He smiled as he threw her words back at her, but lost interest in being amusing as soon as his fingers sank inside her. He pushed them as far as they would go, but she still pressed back, wanting more. The tightness in his gut relaxed.

Withdrawing his fingers from her sheath, he swirled her own juices against her clit, her body writhing against him.

"Wade, I can't wait much longer. Sink that hard cock of yours inside me now."

He didn't stop circling her clit. "I thought you were going to allow me to be in charge this time."

She pulled away from his hands and looked back at him. "Please."

He bent low and kissed her ass. "Okay."

She dropped her head between her arms. "Thank you."

He grabbed the condom from the seat and put it on. Bringing her hips closer, he nudged her in to the position he wanted. Slowly, he entered, pushing, stretching her until he came to her end. He took a deep breath to keep from moving. "Are you good?"

"Oh God, yes." Quiet pants squeezed out around her words, her excitement fueling his own.

He grasped her hips and pressed forward a little more.

Her moan of pleasure was all he needed to hear. He gripped her shoulder with one hand. If he was right about the stagecoach, they were in for the ride of their lives. Pulling his hips back until only his tip was still inside her, he dove back in. He repeated his action, only a bit faster this time. The slight movement of the coach forward and back had him grinning. "Hold on."

Grasping her ass with his other hand, he pulled back and thrust his cock deep inside. The coach pitched.

"Oh wow." Kendra's vocal pleasure was echoed inside her sheath as it squeezed him.

Sharp pleasure shot from his balls to his ass. Relieved it wouldn't hurt her, he thrust again. The jolt of ecstasy as they rocked stole his breath for a second. It was far too good. He drove into her again and again. The motion of the stagecoach making their bodies collide. Each plunge inside her brought him to her cervix then sucked at him as they separated. A cushion of air built inside, adding sensation to every inch of his cock, sending waves of pressure throughout his groin.

He found a rhythm with the stagecoach and held on to her as they rocked and pitched, her mewling sounds of pleasure growing in volume. Then her sheath spasmed and he couldn't hold back. He pounded into her, grasping her hips tight against him as his body jerked with his release.

He collapsed over her, holding on to a seat to keep from crushing her.

Her body gave a tiny shudder. "So that's why I never sold this thing."

He chuckled against her, unable to find the strength for the laugh she deserved. "Don't. I think this has become my favorite spot on the whole resort."

"Hmm, mine too. Did you know it would do that? I mean make it so..."

"Overwhelming? I guessed it might, but had no idea it could be that good."

She sighed. "When I'm with you, I forget everything."

"Then I can't be that boring." He pushed his hips against her ass for emphasis.

"Oh." She turned her head toward him. "I willingly retract my boring remark. However, that *was* perfect."

~~~~~~

Kendra walked into the dining area, thankful she'd had the forethought to build in a generator at least for the main building. As she approached the table, conversation stopped.

Billy jumped up and pulled out a chair. "I gots a special chair reserved just for you." His toothy smile was too adorable to ignore as was his gentlemanly gesture. Had he been taking lessons from Wade?

"Thank you." She sat and her staff went back to eating. Across from her, Wade, sporting a Band-Aid above his eyebrow, gave her a look of approval. She smiled at him in acknowledgement. He had suggested she try to join her staff at least once a week for dinner. It was good advice.

Pouring herself a glass of lemonade from the pitcher on the table, she covertly studied everyone. Billy chatted with Lacey and Powell while Adriana showed Wade her latest earrings. Kendra couldn't ask for a better staff. Maybe a few more, but not better.

Selma bustled through the doorway, a steaming plate of fajita meat in her hands. "It's about time you fucking joined us."

Kendra grinned when her cook piled a large flour tortilla with the seasoned meat and pushed it toward her.

"Now eat."

"I will, in a moment. Please. Sit."

Selma raised her brow but consented to take her seat. Kendra stood, raising her glass. "I have an announcement to make."

Everyone quieted instantly.

"As you know our first guests arrive tomorrow."

"They do?" Powell frowned. "I wish someone had told me."

Oh damn, she must have forgotten to tell him specifically. "I'm sorry. I should have made sure you knew." She glanced at Wade. Another good reason for her to have dinner with her staff since that was the only time they were all together at once.

Powell shook his head. "But we have no electricity. I thought you agreed with the sheriff you would wait another month."

She stared at her security guard. "What? No, I never agreed to do as Sheriff Harper *suggested*." She made sure to add emphasis to the fact Harper hadn't told her she must wait. "And as for the power, thanks to Wade and a friend of his who works for the electric company, we should have it back on in a day or so." No one needed to know the broken pole had never been reported, which meant there might not have been an accident either.

Powell slumped back in his chair and pouted. He was so young. Was she wrong to trust him? "So to clarify..." She smiled at Powell. "We have four couples coming tomorrow. They are well aware of our electricity issue and were thrilled by the discount I gave them. I guess nudists aren't particularly concerned with privacy and all four couples thought a slumber party in the great room was a grand way to open the resort."

Everyone chuckled at that. A few innuendos from Adriana added to the smiles and Kendra clinked her glass with her fork to recapture everyone's attention.

"As we have seen firsthand, by my failure to communicate with Powell, I cannot be everywhere at once, especially with guests here, so I have decided to promote Wade to manager of Poker Flat."

"All right!" Billy yelled. "Guess that mean he be staying more than three months."

Adriana gave him a hug. "Way to go, Cowboy."

"Thanks." Wade took the congratulations humbly.

Powell reached his hand across the table. "Congratulations."

As the two men shook, Selma rose and gave Wade a kiss on the cheek. Kendra relaxed. She'd been afraid her crew would be upset that the newest hired would be promoted. If Wade's plan didn't work and the person trying to keep her from opening didn't try to blackmail him, she still had a great manager. She lifted her glass higher. "To Wade."

Everyone drank to her toast.

Sitting down, she dove into her dinner. She added cheese, lettuce, and a little hot sauce to her fajita and wrapped it up tight. When she took a bite, her gazed locked with Wade's. His knowing grin had her thinking once again he was a bit too full of himself, until the fajita flavors registered on her tongue. Her eyes closed and she couldn't completely stifle the grown of pleasure. Selma needed a raise.

When she opened her eyes, she found Wade's eyebrow cocked. "Good, isn't it?"

Like you. Oh, so that was why he was so smug. "Okay, you were right, I need to eat with my staff more regularly. If not for the camaraderie then for Selma's amazing food." She'd raised her voice with her compliment and nodded to her cook.

Selma grinned. "You are too skinny. Shit, you need to be here every night."

"Maybe I can." Kendra winked at Wade. "Now that I have a manager." Taking another bite of fajita, she looked over her outcasts. In some strange way, they all fit together well, even Mr. Perfect. The fact he had sex with his boss was a serious issue and one they would have to discuss. He gave a whole new meaning to sleeping his way to the top. She smiled before taking another bite.

Wade was on contract now. He was worth the trouble of figuring out how to keep him employed and not have to hide their relationship. She'd talk to her lawyer.

"Time for Tres Leches cake." Selma stood and grabbed Wade's shoulder. "Come, Cowboy. The cake's heavy and my body doesn't need me to carry it. Maybe eat it, but not carry it."

If Selma's cake was even half as good as her churros, Kendra would find room for at least one bite and take the rest with her to her office. There were many benefits to eating with her staff that she'd missed.

Wade graciously stood and followed the cook out.

Kendra ogled him as he left. He really did have an awesome ass. Taking a sip of lemonade, she stared at the last bite of fajita. She was tempted to leave it just to enjoy the cake, but the thought of what Selma would say had her picking it up.

Powell stood. "I'm going to get started on my rounds."

"You don't want to stay for cake?"

"No, I want to be sure everything is set for our guests tomorrow and with a flashlight," he patted the side of his belt, "it will take a lot longer."

"Thank you. And again, I'm sorry I didn't make sure you knew."

He settled the baseball cap more firmly on his head and nodded, then headed outside. He did look quite official in his uniform, almost like the sheriff.

"Here. Everyone better fucking like this. It took me forever." Selma set down plates and forks as Wade placed the large cake on the table.

The cake was quickly distributed and all conversation ceased as the sweet, heavy dessert was devoured.

Kendra ate two bites, but was too full to eat any more, so she picked up her plate as she stood. "Thank you, Selma, for an excellent meal." She turned to everyone else. "Since this building is the only one with power, you are welcome to bunk down here, but you don't have to. Just be sure to grab some linens to put on any couch you might use. Lacey can show you where they are. In the morning, we'll clean up and prepare for our first guests, who shouldn't arrive until after lunch. I'll sleep in my office tonight."

Adriana snickered. "So what's new?"

Lacey piped in. "The sleeping part."

Kendra laughed. They knew her too well. "Point taken. See you all in the morning." She glanced at Wade and waved to Billy then headed for her computer. She still had a few last-minute details to take care of, some of which included how she felt about her new manager and what to do about it.

~~~~~

"Fire me? You're joking, right?" Wade couldn't believe his plan had worked so fast. He'd only been in his casita fifteen minutes.

Just long enough to take off his hat and boots. "Why would she fire me? She just promoted me."

In the soft glow of Wade's lantern, Powell looked uncomfortable, but he reached in his back pocket and pulled out a pair of lavender panties. "I found these in the top drawer of your desk."

They were nothing like the pair Kendra had forgotten in the stagecoach. He'd stuffed those in the bottom draw of his desk until he could return them. Powell only had to go a few drawers down to actually find something incriminating. "So? What about those? They aren't mine."

"Of course they aren't." Powell rolled his eyes. "They're the boss's. I don't know how you got them."

The thought of how Powell had really obtained those had Wade gritting his teeth. Then again, they may not be hers at all. They could be just a pair Powell used to blackmail all the stable managers. Wade tried to relax. "And how do you know they're the boss's?"

"Huh. Uh, well, they… I've seen them in the laundry she left on the washer while I was doing my rounds. And if she knows I found these in your desk, she'll fire you."

Wade turned away, not willing to let the man see the laughter that was sure to be in his eyes. "But you have no proof you found them in my desk."

"I have a picture."

Wade turned at that. "Really? Let me see it."

Pulling the phone from his back pocket, Powell opened the photo. Wade attempted to take the phone to see it.

Powell held on to it. "You can look, but you can't delete it."

He shrugged. "Fine."

The panties shone bright in his top drawer, the rest of the area very dark, probably because Powell had taken the photo tonight by the glow of a flashlight. Wade would bet with the other men, Powell confronted them in the office. He must be desperate to try this stunt.

Wade shrugged. "So? Who's to say you didn't put them in there? I'm not going to quit because you're jealous of my promotion."

The security guard's blank face revealed everything. He couldn't have cared less about the promotion. Then what the hell was his reason for the blackmailing?

"I'm not jealous. If you don't quit, I'll show the boss what I found. I'm trying to give you a chance to take the manly way out."

Something about Powell's phrasing sounded wrong, but Wade couldn't put his finger on what it was. "The manly thing to do would be to confess, not quit. I don't plan to do either."

"But she'll fire you."

"Maybe. Maybe not. I guess we'll see because I'm not quitting."

Powell stuffed the underwear back in his pocket. "Okay, but remember I warned you."

Wade studied the young man. He was nervous and there was a desperate air about him. "Consider me warned."

"Fine, if that's the way you want it." Opening the door to leave, Powell hesitated, then stalked out into the dark.

Wade picked up the battery-powered lantern in his kitchen and strolled into his bedroom. Setting the light on the nightstand, he unbuttoned his shirt. He'd actually been surprised Powell had shown up to blackmail him. He'd written the man off as a suspect. Powell just didn't have the guts for it. And if he was loyal like

Kendra said, then why undermine her with blackmailing the stable managers? Unless he thought the stable managers were a threat to her. Something didn't add up. What was he missing?

Shucking his jeans and underwear, Wade lay down in his bed. As much as he wanted to go to Kendra's office and tell her what happened, he didn't want to risk Powell coming by to tell her the "panty news."

She could come by his place and they could make love in a bed for a change. He grinned. A bed might be too boring for his Kendra. His Kendra? Yeah, he liked thinking of her as belonging to him or rather as his partner. There was very little in her personality that would have her thinking she belonged to anyone. One of the reasons he loved her.

Yeah, he loved her.

He glanced toward the dark windows, almost expecting Dale to jump in and tell him he was nuts for feeling so strongly. Maybe he was nuts, but what he felt was a far cry from his pathetic infatuation with his college girl.

Kendra was a woman, full grown and well able to handle herself. Not to mention handle him. The image of her riding him in the stagecoach had him growing hard.

"Shit." He had to stop thinking about her all together or he'd never fall asleep. Tonight he had a chance for a good night's sleep and he planned on doing so. He had a dozen things to do tomorrow, including setting up some ridiculous saddle covers Kendra had someone make so her guests could ride nude with no danger to their bare skin. Part of him had hoped the naked horseback riding thing wouldn't fly.

But even as he imagined the material fitted on a saddle, he visualized Kendra riding, in all her naked glory except her cowboy boots, her breasts jiggling, her pussy moving back and forth on the new cover.

Ugh. He rolled over. He doubted very much a "good" night's sleep was in store for him.

~~~~~~

Throwing her hat on her table, Kendra sank into her desk chair. The first eight guests of Poker Flat Nudist Resort were now settled in and seemed very impressed. Her staff were giddy with excitement and her own heart still raced. Wade had been a perfect gentleman, not batting an eyelash when he helped one lady out of the wagon who had stripped between the carport and the main building.

Her dream had become a reality.

At the knock on her office door, Kendra stood and smoothed her studded shirt down over her new brown skirt. Admittedly, she was nervous about making the right impression on her first guests. They were all so friendly and not demanding at all, but their views on the resort would weigh a lot. From what she'd read, it was a tight community. "Come in."

Lucinda Richards, a seventy-two-year-old woman with bright white hair and a smile to match peeked her head in. "May I come in?"

"Of course, please, have a seat."

Lucinda walked in naked and set her towel on the wingback chair. She was of average build, a little short, and every wrinkle, blemish, and roll was visible, but she was completely comfortable in her own skin. "I know you have a lot of things on your plate with opening and having no power and such, and you really have thought of everything…"

Kendra smiled. "But…"

"We've been talking, and everyone feels the same way, so I thought I should let you know in case you were unaware."

"Please, Mrs. Richards, tell me. Your feedback will help me make this place everything you want it to be. I built it for you."

"Very well." Lucinda leaned forward as if she were sharing an important secret. "It was strange for us that both you and your manager greeted us with clothes on. All the nudist places we've gone to, either the owner or the manager is nude as well."

"But I was of the understanding employees were to be clothed." A fact Kendra had researched very thoroughly. That's what kept her stomach from sinking at Lucinda's observation.

"Well, that's true, but that only applies to the regular employees. If the owner is on premises then he or she enjoys the naturist lifestyle and that's usually why they open the place. If the owner is an absentee, then the manager gets to enjoy the lifestyle. I've never been to a place that has both until now."

It was all Kendra could do to keep her poker face from taking over. She steepled her hands, bringing her index fingers over her lips, hopefully conveying a thoughtful pose as opposed to revealing the panic racing through her limbs. She was pretty sure if she stood, her knees would shake. She was so sure she'd researched everything. "Do you know why this is how it is?"

Lucinda slapped her hand down on the arm of the chair. "Oh my, yes. It's because only nudists understand nudists. If someone is opening a resort and not comfortable being nude, then they are in it only for the money. Also, how can we trust the owner not to post photos on the website or to keep our privacy if he or she doesn't believe in the lifestyle?"

Kendra did believe in the lifestyle, just not for herself. Dammit, she was in big trouble. "I see your point. I must thank you for bringing this to my attention."

"My pleasure, sweetie." Lucinda rose. "You've created such a beautiful haven for us here. We want you to succeed." She walked over and patted Kendra on the shoulder. "So many of these places go out of business, but we can tell this one is special. See you at the slumber party tonight?"

Kendra forced a smile. "I wouldn't miss it."

"Lovely. See you then." Lucinda picked up her towel and left, her naked butt wiggling with her stride.

"Shit." Kendra pulled the clip out of her hair and ran her hands through it. What the hell was she supposed to do now?

CHAPTER TEN

There was no way Kendra was getting naked. Quickly, she searched the internet, trying to find facts about owners being nude at nudist resorts, but nothing was mentioned.

She very much doubted Lucinda made it up. It was probably one of those unwritten expectations. It did make sense and that's what really bothered her.

For years the idea of owning a nudist resort had simmered in the back of her brain. Ever since Buddy and Ginger had been evicted from the trailer park and then later when they'd been made unwelcome by the home owners' association in their neighborhood and left their dream home for who knows where. They had been the only people in her life to not treat her like trailer trash. They always said it wasn't where a person was born but the size of their heart and what they did with their life that counted. Though nudists, her two friends had the biggest hearts she'd ever encountered.

For her, having a nudist resort wasn't just a niche market, it was about providing a top notch place for a group of people who were not treated fairly. She'd always been a champion of the other side of the tracks, for those not considered mainstream, so she wanted to make a safe haven for nudists. The day she'd gone to visit her friends and found out from their nasty neighbor that "those deviants had been walking around their walled-in backyard naked" and the association "wouldn't put up with their kind living in the community" had been the day she'd begun to dream.

But she never dreamed she'd have to bare all. She couldn't. How would her patrons look at her if they saw her leg? They'd probably vomit up Selma's wonderful food.

She was screwed.

Wade. She needed to talk to him. Sometime in the last couple weeks, she'd come to value his opinion, even though he was perfect. Maybe that's why he fit into her life. The "perfect person" slot in her life had never been filled before. She grinned, despite her anxiousness. Between them, they were bound to find a solution.

She grabbed her hat and headed for the front lobby.

"Kendra."

She halted at Lacey's voice. "Yes."

"You aren't going to believe this."

"What?" She moved around the front desk to view Lacey's computer. "Are those reservations?"

"Yes!" Lacey's squeal of delight was followed by a bear hug, or rather a little bear hug, the petite girl's joy beyond sweet.

"Where did they come from?"

Lacey enlarged a window on her screen. "Here. Some of our guests are raving about Poker Flat already in this forum. If we can keep them happy, I think we will make it."

Kendra took a deep breath. If this was the result from just a few people's opinions, what would be the consequences if those same people thought she was only in it for the money? "I have to go."

"Where are you going?"

Kendra couldn't look at Lacey. There was no way she could give her a smile of encouragement right now. "I have to talk to Wade about an issue one of our guests brought up. I'll be right back."

Pushing her way through the glass doors, she tried to calm her racing heart. How did this happen? How did she not know?

She jumped into her golf cart and drove to the stables. When she peeked around the barn door, she found Wade working on a horse, his naked back to her as he swore up a storm. Just seeing him helped her get control over her nerves. "Wade?"

"What!" He turned around. "Sorry. Didn't mean to snap."

Her curiosity demanded she ask. "What's wrong?"

He moved to his work table and lifted a bottle of water. After taking a few swallows, he wiped his mouth with his arm. "You have your hair down."

"That's a problem? You weren't even looking at me."

"No, I mean—could you put it up? I can't think when you look that delicious."

The fact that he wasn't teasing and completely serious had her heart skipping a beat. Quickly, she wrapped it around itself and pushed it under her hat. "Better?"

He grinned sheepishly. "Yeah. The problem is these damn saddle covers you had made. They aren't tight enough. The minute a person gets on them, they will slip and the rider could fall off."

Her heart sank. She'd thought her design would work. If it didn't, she'd have to disappoint these guests. There had to be something they could do. "Which horse is this?"

"That's Ace. You can't tell them apart?"

She scowled. "It's not as if I'm with them every day like you."

"Whoa, now who's testy?"

She ignored him. "Hello, Ace. I'm just going to check on your saddle, okay?" Gingerly, she moved closer and looked at the cover. It had elastic so it could slip over the saddle easily. At the back it had a drawstring to keep it tight. She found the back hadn't been tied. "Ah, here's the issue. This has to be cinched and knotted. I'd do it, but my knots don't come out as easily as yours."

He stood next to her and pulled the strings. In a heartbeat, he had them secure. Then he looked at her. "I like tying knots."

Her cheeks heated.

"Here, let me lift you up so we can test it."

"Me?" She backed up a step.

"You've never been on a horse, have you?"

She shook her head. "No, but I will eventually."

He stood silent, staring expectantly at her. He wanted to make her feel guilty for not mounting the horse. She didn't guilt easily. "Don't even think about it. Right now we have a big issue to deal with…Mr. Manager."

"Okay. Okay. Let me test this first then as my grandmother says, I'm all ears." Wade put his booted foot in the cushioned stirrup and threw his other leg over.

She backed up to allow him room to maneuver the horse. God, he looked great up there.

He walked the horse out into the parking area and back. When he dismounted, he examined the cover. "I have to admit, it's going to work as long as I keep these beauties down to a walk. But I can't make any guarantees if a horse gets spooked."

"Is that likely?"

"The odds are against it since all of these are dead broke, but even the mellowest horse is going to balk if a rattlesnake crosses its path."

"What is 'dead broke'?"

He took another swallow of water. "It means they are so well trained and mellow they won't start at loud noises or other sudden happenings and are perfect for novice riders. But a horse's instinct regarding dangerous reptiles is a whole other matter."

Another possible problem for her operation she couldn't handle right now. "There's not much I can do about the desert life."

"No, there isn't." He tied Ace to the wall and walked back to her. He didn't stop when he reached her. Instead, he cupped her face and brought his lips to hers.

She wrapped her arms around his neck and kissed him back with every feeling she had for him. When he broke away, she wanted to pull him back. Kissing him made all her troubles disappear. Unfortunately, they still existed when she came back to earth.

Putting a little space between them, Wade leaned back against the barn wall. "Okay. So what new issue do we need to tackle besides Powell trying to blackmail me?"

"What?" Despite the hurt in her heart, somewhere in her brain was a little voice saying, *I told you so.*

Wade nodded. "Yeah, he came to my casita last night. So now we know. Is our problem something worse than deciding how to deal with a traitorous security guard?"

She sighed. "Yes, I think it is. According to my guests, if I want nudists to continue to patronize Poker Flat, one of us must go nude."

"Not a chance." Wade pushed himself away from the wall and strode over to Ace.

That wasn't helpful. "No kidding. I don't want to go nude either. There is a particular part of my body that is completely missing, remember?"

He turned. "That should have nothing to do with it. Your body is perfect just the way it is, but that doesn't mean you should be showing it to every man and woman who comes on the resort. Why is this suddenly a requirement? I thought employees aren't supposed to be nude."

She moved her weight to her right hip. "They aren't, but as it turns out, something that isn't mentioned on the internet is that it's all about the naturist lifestyle. If the owner or manager doesn't participate in it, then the nudists won't come. For them, it is about a life choice, not a financial decision."

Wade untied the saddle cover and pulled it off. "So change your clientele."

"I don't want to change them." She moved around to the other side of Ace so she could see Wade's face. "These people deserve a nice place to vacation like everyone else. For some reason we have family resorts and couples resorts and gay resorts that are all beautiful and first class, but there are very few top-of-the-line places for nudists to go and none with naked horseback riding. Nudists deserve that as much as anyone else."

Wade unbuckled the saddle and pulled it from the horse, his biceps showing her exactly how strong he was. "I don't disagree with you, but someone else can provide that. You have a great destination resort here for anyone."

Something in her gut nudged at her brain. "You said everyone, with the exception of Powell, wanted this resort to succeed."

"They do and it can."

"But you don't want it to succeed as a nudist resort, do you?"

Wade didn't look at her as he pulled some kind of pad off the horse. "I want you to succeed as much as the others. I just can't relate to nudists."

She felt as if she'd been kicked in the stomach by her own horse. "Then what the hell are you doing working here?"

When he didn't answer immediately, it all clicked into place. "Oh, that's right. You are only here as Dale's spy to make sure his business remains successful, not to make sure mine is."

"That's not fair, Kendra."

"Isn't it? Will you get naked for the guests so I can keep my resort the way it is?"

He finally looked at her. "No. I'm not going to be a piece of meat to be judged."

"What? You just stood there and told me my deformity shouldn't matter, but now you're saying your perfect body doesn't deserve scrutiny?"

He raised a brow. "Perfect?"

"Don't change the subject." Her stomach rounded on itself like a desert tumbleweed. "Fine. If you won't go nude then the only way I'm going to keep Poker Flat Nudist Resort open is if I do."

"No." Wade moved around the horse so fast, she had no time to back away. He gripped her upper arms. "No. I don't want anyone seeing you."

Her head spun. "Why?"

"I don't want anyone making advances. Shit, my gut tightens up at the thought of another man just looking at you in the nude."

She looked up at the barn roof and counted to five. "It's not about sex, Wade. It's about being natural." Damn, now she sounded like them. "If you won't do it then I have to or I'll lose all I've worked for."

"Don't."

"I have no choice. I told you. The success or failure of this resort depends on me. I should never have asked you."

His hands gripped her harder. "I can't let you."

"You have no say in the matter."

A shadow came across the barn door. "Take your hands off her." Sheriff Harper stood with his hand resting on the gun at his hip.

Wade's hands loosened but he didn't let go. "This is none of your concern."

"If it has to do with you then it is my concern. I'm here to take you in for questioning."

Wade dropped his hands. "What?"

She stepped in front of him. "He can't go. I have guests. I need my resort manager."

Wade stalked forward, his bearing confrontational. "What did you want to question me about?"

"I have evidence of theft." Harper moved his gaze to her.

Wade shifted into the sheriff's line of sight. "You wouldn't be talking about a pair of ladies underwear, would you?"

Harper's startled look gave him away before he stared hard at Wade.

She stared at Wade as well and then it dawned on her. Wade said Powell tried to blackmail him. It must have been with the panties she'd left behind the other night and when that didn't work, he claimed theft. "Sheriff, I don't think there is any reason to bring Wade in. The fact is, I left those panties behind." She wrapped her arm around Wade and let out her breath when he reciprocated.

Harper's face turned red and he cleared his throat. "Be that as it may, someone has filed charges and Mr. Johnson will need to come with me if he wants to clear his name."

"I can come too."

Harper's face lightened. "That would be fine."

"No, you stay here." Wade turned her to face him. "You have guests. Just don't do anything I wouldn't do." He stared hard at her and she closed off all expression.

"Good point." She looked over her shoulder at Harper. "Sheriff, if you need a statement from me, I can come down anytime when my manager is here."

"Let me get my shirt." Wade pulled away and strode into the tack area.

She approached the sheriff. "I'm sorry for this misunderstanding. I'll send Wade out to the golf cart in a minute."

Harper appeared ready to argue, but there really wasn't anything he could say. "I'll be right here."

She forced a smile. "Thank you."

As soon as he turned, she ran to where Wade tucked in his shirt. "It's Harper."

"What's Harper?"

"He's my saboteur. He's been using Powell to do his dirty work. I'd bet money on it."

Wade eyed her shrewdly. "You may be right. There was something Powell said last night that reminded me of a kid parroting a parent. It was like something Harper would say. Do me a favor and call Dale and tell him where I am in case we are dealing with a crooked sheriff."

"I will. I will also be interrogating a certain security guard."

Wade pulled her close. "Wait for me to be with you. I don't want anything to happen to you."

"Including losing my business?"

"Kendra."

She put her finger on his lips. She was still angry with him for not supporting her nude guests, but her fear he might end up in some desert wash with a bullet in his back overwhelmed her. If Harper was a bad cop, that could very well happen. "Be careful."

He gave her a kiss that left her lightheaded. "I will."

~~~~~

Kendra put down the phone and leaned back in her chair, relief making her shake a little. Her fear had escalated as the hours ticked by and she'd come to one clear decision. She loved Wade Johnson more than a poker player loved his chips and she needed to find a middle ground between her resort and him.

"What happened?" Adriana leaned forward in the wingback chair on the other side of the desk, oblivious to her own nakedness.

"Dale said Wade's safe and he's not in jail."

"And…?"

Kendra sat forward, feeling more settled than she had in the last two weeks. "Harper is now being investigated by Internal Affairs and has been suspended."

"That's a bit harsh for a trumped-up theft charge."

"Oh, it's much more than that. The electric company discovered the pole had been halfway cut with a chainsaw and since no accident report was ever filed, it clearly pointed to the sheriff. Wade also told them about Game and Fish having to come out here because of Harper. When Wade also promised them a witness, the department decided to take it seriously."

Adriana's eyes grew round with curiosity. "Who's the witness?"

"Powell. But we haven't spoken to him, so keep that under your hat."

"Of course. So have you decided if—"

A knock on the door interrupted Adriana.

Kendra's stomach clenched. She couldn't handle any more suggestions from guests right now. "Come in."

Leonard, Lucinda's husband, poked his head in and Kendra stood, making herself smile. "Hi, Mr. Richards. What can I do for you?"

He frowned. "I was sitting on the patio of my casita, enjoying a drink when I noticed someone working on the bridge across the creek. We have friends joining us in a few days and I was just wondering if it would be repaired in time for them to cross over."

Someone working on the bridge? There was nothing wrong with her bridge. A shiver rode up her back. "Oh yes. The bridge is new. We are simply making a few small adjustments. In fact, I was just heading down there now to see how it was going."

Leonard broke into a smile. "Great. I thought so, but the Mrs. was concerned so I thought I'd better check."

"No problem. I'm glad you asked." She kept her smile until Leonard had nodded and closed the door.

"What the hell?" Adriana stood. "That bridge is brand new. It doesn't need repair."

Kendra grabbed her hat. "You and I both know that. I'm going to investigate."

"I'm going with you."

"No!" At Adriana's stunned expression, Kendra lowered her voice. "No, I need someone here to be sure none of the guests venture down there until I find out what's going on."

Adriana scowled. "Fine. But if you're going alone, take your gun."

"I don't think I need a gun."

Adriana's hands found her hips. "Yes, you do. Do you remember those college boys from town who decided to graffiti the garage after it was built?"

Kendra's throat closed. She'd already forgotten that episode, mainly because she didn't want to remember the hateful sayings on the metal structure. "Good point." Bending, she opened her bottom drawer and pulled out her Smith and Wesson 9mm. She'd learned early in her career that winning money meant attempted robberies. She just never expected to have to use it once she owned her own spread.

Slipping the gun into the pocket of her skirt, she moved past Adriana. "Remember, don't let any guest come down to the bridge. I don't need this place being known for vandalism."

"Okay."

Once down the hall, she was glad she didn't have to talk to any patrons as she exited the building. She felt as if she held the winning hand in a high stakes game and the fire alarm just went off. Jumping into her golf cart, she drove down the path, being sure not to send up any dust. She didn't want anyone to know what was happening except her.

A part of her wished Wade was back, but the other part was happy he was making sure Harper never bothered them again. As the bridge came into view, she could clearly see a man in jeans and t-shirt using a sledgehammer on the bridge.

"Fuck you. You bastard." Rage tore through her as she drove around the corner losing sight of the man for a moment. Adrenaline rushed through her veins while she contemplated whether to shoot to kill or just wound. The former was her preference. Fuck. If she shot him, all the guests at the resort would know something was wrong.

Gritting her teeth with frustration, she turned the corner on the last switchback and lessened the pressure on the pedal, letting the quiet golf cart roll to a stop. Deciding surprise was her best move, she slowly left the cart, never taking her eyes off the man.

Just then he moved to angle the swing of the sledgehammer and she couldn't contain her surprise. "Harper?"

At the sound of her voice, he turned, missing his mark with the tool. "You."

He dropped the sledgehammer and bounded toward her. His face was drawn with rage, appearing almost skull-like, his breathing harsh.

She slipped her hand into her pocket just as his hands bit into her upper arms. "You." The black of his pupils had blotted out the color of his eyes. "You ruined my career, my county, my nephew."

She had the gun in her grip but kept her hand in her pocket. "What? What are you talking about? *You* sabotaged my resort."

"A naked resort," he spat. What had been an annoying, pathetic sheriff was replaced by a zealous fanatic. "It took me awhile to put it together, but I finally figured it out. You built this place for orgies. All that talk about nature and shit, was you pretending to the planning committee. We don't want your kind in our county, messing with our kids' heads, twisting their morals. I looked into your background. You're just a piece of white trash with big boobs."

The old words didn't hurt anymore. She was done with being judged for a childhood and anatomy she'd had no control over. Screw him. With her arms pinned, she couldn't slap him, so she spit in his face.

He laughed, throwing his head back, allowing her to see around him and catch movement on the path behind him. *Wade.*

When Harper finished laughing, he sneered at her. "You white cunt. You want to trade spit with me that bad?"

Without warning, his mouth came down on hers, bruising her lips. Fury rose in her throat as he forced his tongue into her mouth.

She bit it...hard.

He jerked his head away. "God damn slut." Letting go of her arm, he lifted his hand to slap her even as she pulled her weapon from her pocket.

CHAPTER ELEVEN

Harper screamed, grasping his leg as he crumpled to the ground before Kendra could pull the trigger.

Wade stood behind him, the sledgehammer in his hand.

She relaxed her finger. "Thanks for the help."

He pointed to the gun in her hand and raised an eyebrow. "Would you have killed him?"

She looked at the sheriff, his leg at an odd angle and blood already seeping through his jeans. She searched her heart for the answer, Harper's words, his kind, had etched a scar deep in her soul. "Maybe."

"Glad I arrived when I did." He lowered the sledgehammer, his gaze going to the gun still pointed in his direction. "I'd rather you didn't go to jail."

She tried to change her facial expression, but she couldn't. "For killing a crooked cop?"

Wade shrugged. "He's still a cop…at the moment."

Her anger and disgust at Harper loosened its hold on her and she returned the gun to her pocket.

Wade glanced down at the unconscious sheriff and stepped around him. "Are you okay?"

"Yeah. He wasn't the first to treat me like that. My first boss taught me early."

Wade's hands curled into fists and she stared at them. Taking one of his hands, she kissed it. "It's okay. Haven't you heard, what doesn't kill you makes you stronger."

"Ah shit." Wade's arms came around her in a tight hug and the defensive shell around her emotions split.

She hugged him back with all her strength, the wonder of being comforted too new to process at once. It simply felt good.

He leaned back to look at her. "Hey. I'm proud of you."

"Why?"

The right side of his lips lifted just a bit. "You are one strong woman."

She shrugged, not feeling very tough now that she'd melted into him. She rested her face against his chest, inhaling the scent of masculine soap and hay.

Harper moaned and Wade sighed. "Guess I'll be running a certain sheriff back to the department, though I may have to stop at the emergency room first. I'm sure at least one leg is broken. He's lucky. I actually aimed for his head, but was so angry I couldn't see straight." He gave her a self-deprecating smirk. "Will you be okay while I'm gone?"

She nodded against his chest, but she didn't want to move away from him. He was everything that was good and for once she believed she deserved that.

He kissed the top of her head. "I'll be back as soon as I can."

She sighed, unwilling to let him go. "That's fine. I have guests to see to." Finally, she lifted her face and gazed into his warm eyes.

He lowered his mouth to hers and kissed her gently. She opened to him, loving his tender exploration of her mouth.

He pulled away too soon. "Are you sure you're okay?"

She gave him a tentative smile. It was hard. "Yes. Now go." She made herself step away from him. "Adriana is going to be worried sick and I need to get Billy down here to assess the damage, so we can repair this right away."

He took her hand and walked her back to her golf cart. "All right. I'll fill in the sheriff's office on this incident. Are you going to want to press charges?"

She got in and looked up at him. "You bet I will."

"Good."

She squeezed his hand still in hers and let him go. "I'll see you when you get back." She made herself start the cart and turn away from him. She had a lot to do and a very important decision to make. Hanging around with her perfect cowboy only delayed the inevitable.

She made her way up to the resort, trying to focus on her to-do list, but she couldn't stop thinking of Wade's comforting hug. Damn, she was pathetic.

~~~~~~

Adriana smiled. "You're going to keep your hat and boots on, aren't you?"

Kendra tensed. "Yeah." She had changed into her tall cowboy boots, which should hide most of her damaged calf. There was no way she'd take them off.

She glanced at the clock. Wade still hadn't returned, which made her less comfortable with what she was about to do. She would have liked to give him a heads-up. "Thank you for doing this with me."

Adriana winked. "My pleasure. I'll go see if everyone is finished with dessert while you undress."

"Sounds good."

After the door closed on her naked bartender, Kendra stood. She'd learned she wasn't quite acceptable soon after receiving the coyote bite. Whether it was her trailer trash childhood, her deformed leg or what she did for a living, she would always be an outsider. Besides, going nude was far too beyond the pale for Wade to accept. This was her problem and she preferred to stand on her own two feet anyway. So if she wanted her dream to live, she would have to get naked. Then, somehow, she would have to remember to smile and react while being incredibly embarrassed.

She shook herself. One problem at a time. First, she had to get naked.

"This is for you Buddy and Ginger." Quickly, before she lost her resolve, she stripped off her shirt and bra. Dropping the brown skirt she'd worn to greet the guests, she stepped out of it. Without hesitating, she pulled her panties down over her boots and threw them on her chair. They were a new pair, with pretty pink lace edging. She'd have to remember to retrieve those tonight. It was bad enough she had one traveling pair of underwear. She didn't need two.

The door opened and Adriana bopped in, closing it behind her. "I had a brilliant—whoa, look at you. You're stacked!"

Heat started in her cheeks and moved down her chest. "Yeah, I've noticed." She picked up the towel she would sit on in the great room.

Adriana moved closer. "Honey, I'm sorry. I didn't mean to embarrass you. It's just that you would have made a fortune in a brothel."

She rolled her eyes. "Thanks, I think."

"I'm not helping, am I? How about this?" Adriana pulled a deck of cards out from behind her back.

"We can't play strip poker, Adriana. We don't have any clothes on."

"No, no, no. I have them interested in playing Texas Hold'em. When I told them you were Night Owl Lowe, they couldn't wait for me to find a deck of cards."

Texas Hold'em? If she was playing poker, she wouldn't have to react. "You are a genius." She hugged Adriana to her then stepped back quickly. "Okay, that was weird."

Adriana grinned. "Not for me. Men, women, multiples, even handcuffs, I'm game for anything."

"Okay, too much information. Let's just stick to poker. We're going to need chips to bet with. I refuse to take money from my guests."

Adriana grinned. "Not a problem. Selma made a new batch of churros and I have Lacey cutting them into thin slices. If guests happen to eat their money, it's not our fault."

Kendra was so grateful she wanted to cry, but that wasn't exactly the reaction her friend was looking for. "Thank you for all this. I couldn't have come this far without you."

"Just remember me when you become famous…again." Adriana winked and sauntered toward the door. "Are you ready? Do you have your towel?"

She took a deep breath, clasping her towel close to her chest. "Let's do this."

Adriana opened the door and they made their way down the short hall toward the great room.

If Lacey had finished making the "chips," she would be gone as would Selma. Billy always retired right after dinner and Wade wasn't back, which left only Powell. If the security guard did his job tonight instead of snooping where he didn't belong, then none of her staff would see her, except Adriana.

As they turned the corner, she scanned her eight naked guests. Two men stood by the cold fireplace chatting with drinks in their hand. One woman showed another how to play poker and a couple counted out the churro chips. Lucinda and her husband approached. "I thought I recognized you from somewhere. Now I know. I can't believe you're *the* Night Owl. You know you're much prettier in person."

Kendra pasted on a smile and moved her weight to her right hip. "They do say TV adds ten pounds."

Lucinda patted her tummy. "Menopause will add more, but as long as Leonard is happy with me, I'm happy."

Leonard looked at his wife like he would give her the moon if he could.

Kendra's smile started to feel real. "I think, Mrs. Richards, you are a very lucky lady."

Lucinda batted her hand, but Leonard wouldn't let her off the hook so easily. "Don't let her fool you, Ms. Lowe. I was very lucky to meet Lucinda. If it wasn't for her, I wouldn't be here today."

"Really?"

"Yes, I'd be alone in a nursing home somewhere and worst of all, I'd be dressed."

Adriana and Lucinda chuckled while Kendra nodded as if she understood. She didn't, not really.

Lucinda grasped her hand. "Would you do the honor of playing poker with us? Adriana said you might be willing to. It would be such a great story to tell the others at our club."

"Oh, you have a card club?"

"No, no. Our nudist club. We play Texas Hold'em every Saturday afternoon there. So don't go easy on us. We know what we're doing." Lucinda winked and Kendra relaxed a little more. No one had commented on her appearance and no one had stared at her. "I would be happy to play."

"Oh, good." Lucinda clapped her hands once and spun around to face the others. "She'll play."

Cheers greeted that news, and Kendra was quickly ushered to the head of the coffee table.

For the first few hands, she had a hard time concentrating, just not comfortable without clothes. She surreptitiously glanced at her fellow players' bodies. Is that what they did? Look but not be obvious about it? They seemed more concerned with their cards than her.

All eight of her guests were older than she, probably sixties and seventies. They were all shapes and sizes and one man had a long scar down the center of his chest while a woman to the right had a brown stain covering her entire right arm and half of her breast. Attractiveness didn't seem to have any place in the nudist lifestyle. It was such a freeing thought, but was it real?

When she lost a large pot of churro chips, her competitive instincts took over and she refocused her attention on winning. Everyone was having fun, talking and joking. Adriana made sure they all had drinks, though she wasn't officially working.

Kendra was concentrating on a particularly good hand when the sound of the front lobby door opening distracted her. Immediately, she tensed. Whoever it was, it wouldn't be someone she wanted to see her naked. She was completely comfortable with the nudists now, but a staff member besides Adriana wouldn't be good.

As the footsteps came closer to the corner of the great room, her heart sank. It had to be Wade.

A moment later, he appeared and halted. She looked at him as he scanned the room, taking everything in. When his gaze rested on her, his jaw tightened. He shook his head slowly, as if she'd disappointed him. Then his hands formed fists and he turned on his heel, heading back the way he'd come.

"Do you call, Kendra?"

"What? Oh yes, I call." She wanted to rush out after him and apologize, but she wasn't sure what for. Hurting him? Doing what she thought was right even if he didn't agree?

"Kendra?" Adriana snapped her fingers in front of her face. "Are you all right? That's your pot."

Her gut told her she had to talk to him sooner rather than later. "Go ahead and split it among everyone. I have to get back to work."

"Already?" Lucinda whined, having raked in the second highest number of churros, although only because her husband kept eating his.

"Yes, I'm afraid so." She managed to smile kindly before standing.

She started out but Lucinda called her back. "Don't forget your towel."

"Thanks. I'll just—get it now." She returned, not sure if leaving it behind would have been the right etiquette. She'd been about to say she'd get another. There was so much more to learn about her clientele, and it wasn't all on the internet. Hopefully, her sacrifice tonight would help Poker Flat's budding reputation.

As she reached the door to her office, her newest quandary hit her. She needed to see Wade, but should she put her clothes on or leave them off? If she put them on, he might be pissed she covered her body in front of him but not the guests. If she approached him naked, he might look at her in disgust and that would absolutely devastate her.

"Damn, this sucks." She grasped the towel to her chest as if it could help, and then it did. Wrapping the towel around her, she strode outside to find Wade. The question was where would he be. Getting in her golf cart, she drove to the barn just in case. Sure enough, a cart was parked outside and a dim light shone from inside.

She called out as she approached. "Wade?"

"What?"

She couldn't see into the back of the barn as the lantern was near the entrance, but she could hear a horse moving in a stall. "Wade, are you back there?"

He growled, "Yeah."

Was this what was meant by facing a lion in his own den? She straightened her shoulders. She owned that den so this lion better come out. "We need to talk."

"Why?"

Ugh. His one-word answers pissed her off. "Because you're angry and I want to know why."

The sound of boots hitting the concrete floor reached her before he emerged. His face made her wish she could talk to the darkness again, his scowl so much harsher with the shadows.

"You really have no idea why I'm angry? Come on, Kendra, you're smarter than that."

"And so are you. I've spent two years working on this resort for nudists. I researched everything I could, sank millions of dollars into its development and find out at the last minute if I don't go nude, all I worked for could go down the drain. So I get naked and you stomp off."

Leaning against the opposite wall, Wade folded his arms across his chest, his scowl deeper, if that were possible. "First, I didn't *stomp* off. Second, you're taking the word of a few guests that not being naked would kill your enterprise without giving it a chance. Third, if it really didn't work out, you could always open the place up to clothed people. Families would love this setting, but you won't even consider that. And fourth, you knew how I felt about you going nude and you did it anyway."

She folded her arms, mimicking him. What she really wanted to do was punch him as the real reason he was upset revealed itself. He was angry she hadn't done what he wanted. "Yes, I did know how you felt, but you aren't the law. I respect your opinion, but in the end, it's my choice and I chose to go nude. Now you don't have to. You should be relieved."

"Dammit! I don't want anyone seeing you." Wade stalked toward her. "It's just not right. I want you to myself."

Her heart did somersaults at where he was headed. "Why?"

He halted, looking away.

"Wade? Why do you want me to yourself?"

He finally met her gaze. "I just do."

She shook her head. "Really? That's all. Well that's not good enough. You need to go all-in on this one. In fact…" She tore off the towel. "I'm willing to bare my body and my heart. I love you. *I* want you to myself because *I* love you."

His gaze moved from her face to her breasts and lower. When he raised it again, desire, hurt, and anger collided. "Then don't do this anymore." He pointed to her nakedness. "If you love me, you'll respect my preference to keep you covered."

Her eyes watered. She'd given him a chance, but he'd brushed it and her away. Mr. Perfect wasn't so perfect after all. "If you cared for me, you would support my nudity for the sake of my dream."

Wade shook his head. "I won't fold on this issue."

She looked down to wrap her towel around herself again, hiding her teary eyes. When she raised her head, her stoic face was firmly in place. "A good poker player knows when to fold and when to stay in the game." She spun, intending to return to her cart.

"Kendra, I'm not a poker player." Wade's hand on her arm had her stopping.

She didn't turn around. "No, you're not." He was far too good for that.

He sighed. "I just can't."

She nodded once and pulled away. "You should probably call Dale and tell him I need employees who are okay with naked people strolling around, including their boss."

As she settled in the golf cart, she glanced at Wade's silhouette in the barn doorway. Gritting her teeth against the pain in her heart, she kept the tears at bay and drove down the path. She had barely reached the main building when the first sob overtook her.

She doubled over. Tears streamed down her face. She rocked as the hurt speared through her, eating her insides. She'd made the mistake of falling for one of the good ones. She should have known. She and Wade came from completely different backgrounds and had different values. Wade would never understand.

Her towel soaked in her tears but it couldn't take away her pain. A pain caused by reaching "beyond her sphere." That's what her ex–husband had said, but he'd meant his social standing. She'd been good enough to distract his supervisors with her breasts and help him get promoted, but when he needed to find his own rich clients, he'd needed a wife from a much higher level of society. Wade also lived in a completely different sphere than she did. His was the one without misfits or outcasts or second chances.

When she could finally catch her breath without sobbing on the exhale, she looked at the main building. The floor-to-ceiling windows of which she was so proud revealed the light and fun inside. She couldn't be there.

She turned the golf cart and drove to her dark little house set slightly apart from the staff casitas.

Letting herself in, she was anxious for the numbing relief of sleep.

She stilled at the sight of light flickering in her bedroom. What the hell?

CHAPTER TWELVE

Kendra froze, but her blood heated with fury. Someone was in her bedroom. And her gun was back in her office. Shit.

She needed a weapon. Something heavy could work. Where had she left the tools she'd used the other day when she put together her bookcase? Probably still on the floor. With her luck tonight, she'd trip over them.

The flickering light hit the living room, reflecting off the hammer sitting on the top shelf before it moved to another spot in her bedroom. Leaving the outside door open, she quietly moved to her only choice for a weapon. Grasping it firmly in hand, she tiptoed toward the open doorway. Her heart pounded, making her breathing speed up, but her years of poker kept her hand steady.

The person opened a drawer in her nightstand, the flashlight illuminating the contents inside. She'd heard someone once say offense was the best defense. She doubted that held true for a woman in a towel with a hammer in hand. Aiming for her bedroom door, she slammed the hammer into it.

The noise sounded like a gun shot and the person in her room yelled as the flashlight fell to the floor. "Don't shoot! Don't shoot!"

Crouching, she grabbed the light and shined it on her burglar. "Powell? What the hell are you doing here?"

"I'm sorry, boss. I had to. He said he'd get me in. I needed something more."

She shook her head, even though Powell wouldn't be able to see her with the light in his face. Then again, he wouldn't know she didn't have a gun, either. "What are you babbling about?"

"My uncle. He promised to get me into the police academy if I made problems for you. I didn't want to, but you always said we should follow our dreams."

"Not at the expense of others or by participating in illegal activities." She sighed. "Who's your uncle?"

Powell pursed his lips.

"You better tell me right now, or I'll have you arrested."

His shoulders fell. "Sheriff Harper."

What? That's what Harper had been raving about. He thought she had corrupted his law-breaking nephew? The man was certifiably nuts. "Do you really think he would help you become a policeman when he was having you break the law?"

Powell thought for a moment. "He said he would."

"Well, he isn't anymore."

Powell's face fell. "Please, boss. Don't turn me in. Don't tell him you caught me or he'll make sure I never get accepted."

She'd known Powell was young when she'd seen him that day in court, but for an expert hacker he was very naïve. "Harper won't be doing anything for anyone for a while. He's been suspended while under investigation. I'm afraid you hitched your horses to the wrong wagon."

Powell looked like he would cry and there was no way she wanted to see that. She changed the subject to avoid an embarrassing scene. "What were you doing in my room?"

"I was supposed to take a bra of yours and leave it in one of the casitas so it looked like you had sex with one of the male guests."

Adrenaline rushed through her at how close she'd come to losing the goodwill of her first patrons. That, of anything so far, would have done it. Now, what to do with Powell? "Come on. You're leaving Poker Flat right now."

"What? No, boss, please. I can't lose this job."

"Powell, I may give second chances, but there are no third chances from me. Let's go." She motioned with the flashlight. "If you leave peacefully, I'll give you two weeks' pay as a going-away gift, not that you deserve it. You can come back in the morning to pick up your belongings and your last check."

The young man bowed his head, sniffing. "Okay."

As he walked by her, she grabbed the baseball cap off. "I'll be keeping this."

His hand made for his head but she was too fast. His shoulders slumped and he wiped at his nose with his sleeve.

Nudging his back with the head of the hammer, she pushed him forward. "Come on. You drive."

~~~~~~

Wade waved goodbye to his first three customers. They had to be old enough to be his grandparents, but had acted like children on the trail ride, exclaiming after every cactus, view and horse. They did love the horses. He had to like people who loved horses.

He'd give Kendra credit for that too. She'd done her research and granted these people the chance to do something they'd always wanted to do, but in a safe environment. The slow gait of the horse combined with the padding she'd designed protected them. Even so, they'd still used their towels. He grinned.

The guests' golf cart passed one heading toward him and his heart jerked at the hope it was Kendra, but it was only Billy. Turning, he strode inside. He had four horses to take care of and didn't have time for Billy if the man was drunk again.

Starting with Sam, Wade removed all his riding gear and walked him into his stable. He still couldn't believe Kendra had gone nudist on him even after she knew he was dead set against it. Seeing her sexy body amongst all that naked flesh had his dreams going wild last night.

He made himself focus on Buca, finally getting her stripped and into her stall. What did the guests think of Kendra's body? He hated the idea they had viewed her and made some kind of judgment. Maybe they had dreams too.

After unsaddling Sundancer, his curiosity finally got the best of him and he strolled over to look into the parking area. Billy stood next to his cart talking to himself.

"Billy, what are you doing?"

The older man jumped as if caught red-handed, but came forward anyway. "I were trying to decide what to say to you."

The man's frown and obvious nervousness made Wade more curious. "Since when do you have to choose your words around me? Just say what you want to say. It's that easy. But come inside out of the sun so I can finish taking care of the horses."

Billy followed him and sat on a hay bale, but still didn't say a word. At least he wasn't drunk this time.

Wade shrugged and finished with Sundancer then started on Ace.

"What does you did?"

Billy's sudden question caught Wade off guard. "I'm not sure what you mean. I just gave three people a trail ride and now I'm taking off the saddles."

"No." Billy dug his hands into the hay. "I means what does you did to upset Miss Kendra."

Wade tensed, but saw no reason to hide his feelings. "I told her I didn't want her to go nude."

"Why?"

"Because it's not right."

Billy's nose scrunched, making the lines around it disappear into the wrinkles under his eyes. "But those people you took on the ride was naked. Why that all right?"

Wade relaxed. "Because they're nudists."

"But Miss Kendra run a nudist resort. Why can't she be nude?"

"Because I don't want anyone else to see her without any clothes on. Do you want people to see her nude?"

"Sure, if that what she want. Why doesn't you want people to sees her?" Billy's stare was too focused.

Wade sighed. "You're asking a lot of questions."

"And you is not answering them."

Wade put down the feed he'd been about to take to Sam and gave Billy his full attention. "Okay, I don't want other people to see Miss Kendra because I like her...a lot. And I want her all to myself."

"Good." The old man grinned. "So you does want her to succeed, right?"

He raised a brow. "Yes. So?"

Billy shrugged. "So that mean you would does anything to help her."

Wade shook his head. "It's more complicated than that." More than Billy could possibly understand.

"Why is you working on a nudist resort if you doesn't like nudists? All of us come here knowin' exactly what she plan. What make you think she change that now? Because you doesn't likes them?"

"I—"

Billy stood. "You gots to figure out if you is here for the right reasons and exactly how much you 'likes' Miss Kendra because the rest of us is in this for the long haul. And if the only reason you is breaking Miss Kendra's heart are because you is a prude, then you needs to leave sooner rather than later."

Wade stared at the old man. Shit. He was getting dressed down by a drunk.

"Don't looks at me like that." Billy wagged his stubby finger. "Yeah, we all a bit tainted but we is pure of heart and loyal. You be pretty on the outside, but we still waiting to sees how good that heart of yours are. You best decide your int-int—what you wants and decides fast. Miss Lacey hear Miss Kendra on the phone asking Mr. Dale at that there temp agency to finds her a new security guard and stable manager."

Wade's heart skipped a beat. "She wants to replace me?"

"She are making it a requirement that employees is comfortable with people walking around nude. I think she enjoying it a little."

Wade had no idea what to think about that. Kendra had been pretty shy about anyone seeing her leg.

"Plus, after she gone and catch Powell in her room last night, she need a new security guard."

"Powell was in her room?" Wade stepped closer, his hands fisting of their own accord. "What happened?"

Billy put his hands out in front of him. "Hey, it weren't me. I just hear a hammer were involved and she took that security cap he love so much. We kept quiet while he comes back this morning for his things, but rumors is flying now." Billy grinned, obviously enjoying the stories that were circulating.

Wade should have been there with her. Instead, he'd been sulking in the barn.

"Anyways, I just thought you likes to know you ain't gots much time to decide. Thinks on it. You knows what they says. 'If you doesn't go nude, you must be a prude.'" The old man chuckled, showing his missing tooth. "See you at dinner."

"Thanks, Billy."

The old man nodded and shuffled outside then stopped and looked back. "You knows about that thing you has about others seeing Miss Kendra naked?"

Wade lifted an eyebrow, wary. "Yeah?"

"Does you ever think how she feel if you was naked too?" The sly devil winked and then continued on his way.

No, he hadn't thought about what it would be like for Kendra if he was naked because he'd never planned on getting naked in public.

He hadn't called Dale either, even though Kendra had asked him to. He wanted to give her time to cool down first, but that wasn't happening. If she truly loved him, wouldn't she at least give them a chance?

Yeah, but last night he'd been an ass, in shock at seeing her sitting naked among a bunch of other naked people despite the fact he'd asked her—okay, told her—not to. His anger had taken over. From the first moment he'd met her, it was obvious she would never be the dependent type and he liked that, so why did he want her to do as he said now?

He shook his head and picked up the feed. He had a lot to think about.

~~~~~~

Kendra reviewed the photos her guests had emailed of them on the resort. They told her she needed to show naked people on her website, otherwise the place would appear sterile. Four of them didn't care if they were on the internet and had the others take the pictures.

She grinned at the one with Lucinda's husband doing a cannonball in the pool. Another showed three of them toasting at the bar. There was one that had particularly good lighting with them sitting in the conversation pool. The next showed a couple riding naked on horseback. They had come back glowing after that. She clicked on the following photo and Wade stared at her, his arm around Lucinda's shoulders.

That was the last photo she wanted to see. What would he think if he could see her now, sitting behind her desk naked as the day she was born, except for her boots? She never took those off in public. Quickly, she moved to the next photo. It was a cute one of two ladies giving Billy a kiss on each cheek. At least she still had her outcasts, although she'd lost one.

"Hey, Kendra." Adriana stood in the doorway. "You have to see this."

Her bartender had been stopping in throughout the day, completely charmed by their guests. "I'm a little busy right now."

"Not too busy for this. Seriously, you need to come."

It couldn't hurt to stretch her legs a bit. She'd been sitting at the computer for over two hours. "Okay." Rising, she threw on her cowboy hat and stepped outside her office. "What do I need to see?"

"This way." Adriana pulled her by the hand and she twisted away. "I'm a big girl. I can follow you without getting lost in my own resort."

Adriana laughed but continued past the front desk to the edge of the great room.

Kendra stopped before Adriana did. Standing next to the fireplace chatting with Lucinda and Leonard was Wade. A very naked Wade. A very naked, hot, muscular, sexy Wade in cowboy boots and hat. She had to stifle the urge to drag him into her office and ride him.

Lucinda distracted her when the older lady patted Wade's hard forearm. The woman was flirting outrageously, which was adorable. But what if it was a gorgeous Hispanic young woman like Adriana? How adorable would it be then? Was that what Wade meant when he'd said he didn't want anyone else looking at her? Probably. She had to admit, he'd seen that problem before she did.

Then what was he doing? He was supposed to be opposed to the whole nudist concept.

Lucinda spotted her. "Hey, it's the Night Owl. She finally emerged from her nest." The woman laughed at her wit, but Kendra didn't even smile as she gazed into Wade's eyes. They crinkled at the corners as he lifted his lips in a warm smile. Then he mouthed three words. *I love you.*

Her weight settled on her right hip as her insides melted into a puddle of mush that surely everyone could see leaking into her boots. She wanted to go to him, but her feet were stuck and she had no strength.

Wade must have perceived her predicament, pretty obvious with all that goo running over the top of her boots by now, and he strode across the room. He stood in front of her, blocking her from the view of everyone. She should thank him for that, but she couldn't make her mouth form the words.

"Can I talk to you in private for a moment?"

She nodded, but still didn't move.

He looked over his shoulder. "We'll be back in a moment, folks. Don't do anything we wouldn't do while we're gone."

The group chuckled and made a few jokes, but Wade linked her arm in his and walked her toward her office.

When they arrived, he closed the door and grasped her face.

She opened her mouth to speak, but his lips came down on hers in a gentle, loving kiss. Oh God. She wrapped her arms around his waist as he played with her tongue, leisurely stroking and sucking.

Eventually, he moved his kisses to the outside of her lips, then her jawline and to a spot behind her ear. She scrunched up her shoulder. "That tickles."

He raised his head and used one hand to take off her hat and throw it on the table. "We need to talk."

Hearing her own words thrown back at her made her nervous, but since his arms were still around her, it couldn't be that bad. "Okay, talk."

He smirked. "I'm sorry. I shouldn't have expected you to give up your dream for me. I was selfish, one of my many faults. You had always been very open about your plans and I knew full well what I was into, but I kept my feelings about it close to the vest and that was wrong."

She studied him, trying to piece together the thought process that had brought him to this point, but she couldn't. "Apology accepted. But you were against getting naked, against nudist resorts. So why are you naked, I mean except for the hat?"

He gave her his full smile and her heart filled with love. "A few naked people and one old coot showed me the error of my judgment." He wiggled his eyebrows. "And it's kind of fun. I didn't have to decide which pair of blue jeans to put on to come over here. As for the hat, I looked strange without it."

Her heart soared and she clasped him around the neck to give him a kiss of her own, plastering her naked body against his. He could never look strange to her. He was perfect. When her mons rubbed against his hard cock, he broke off their kiss. "Whoa, if we're going to be walking around naked, we will need regular private times to take care of this." He looked down at his erection.

"I'll be happy to help with that." She slanted her gaze at him. "I thought you said cowboys never fold."

He looked affronted. "I didn't fold. I just raised the stakes and you called."

She wrinkled her nose. "So why did you raise the stakes? I wasn't bluffing."

"I know, but the pot was well worth winning. I love you, Kendra, Night Owl, whatever. I want to be your number-one misfit if you'll let me."

"It would be my pleasure."

He scooped her up in his arms and laid her on her table. "Hmmm, actually, I think it will be mine."

She laughed, grasping his ass as he leaned over her, his tongue invading her mouth once again. By betting the highest stakes she had, her heart, she'd won the biggest jackpot of her life.

Her very own cowboy.

EPILOGUE

"She's taller than I remember."

Wade grinned. It had taken two weeks, but he'd finally dragged Kendra away from her work to experience her own naked trail ride. The fact that Buddy and Ginger had made a reservation had tipped the scales. Kendra wanted to be sure the experience was perfect, but she was hesitant. "Don't worry, I'll be with you."

She looked doubtful as she eyed Sundancer.

"Come here. I'll show you a tall horse." Taking her by the hand, he brought her out back to where Sage was enjoying the sun in the corral. "You remember Sage, right? Now this is tall." He patted the sturdy Belgian. Sage was the most relaxed horse at the resort but one of the strongest, pulling the guests and their luggage in the wagon. Wade would never tire of the patrons' enjoyment of the ride or the gasps when the resort came into view.

She pressed her naked body against his side and he wished they were skin to skin, but he was working, so he was fully clothed.

Luckily, Kendra had hired Jorge back. His fight had been with Sheriff Harper when Jorge defended Kendra and he was willing to return now that he wouldn't be blackmailed anymore. That pleased Dale. It changed his record with Poker Flat Nudist Resort to one hire being promoted, one staying and two leaving. He could live with that since there shouldn't be any more strange occurrences. Unfortunately, the old stable manager wouldn't arrive for two more days, which meant Wade still had stable duty.

She squirmed against him. "Okay, you made your point."

He moved her closer. "Go ahead, you can pet her. She likes people."

Kendra's hesitancy lasted less than a minute. She stroked the horse's side and her smile appeared again, an expression he loved getting used to.

"She reminds me of the beer commercial."

He stroked Sage too, and the horse looked back to nuzzle his arm. "Those are a different breed, but you're right in that she is big like that. So are you ready to try Sundancer?"

"Yes."

After giving Sage a final pat, he led Kendra back to her waiting Arabian. His predecessor had done well in researching trail riding horses for the area. All Wade had to do was pin down the ones he liked the most. He still needed at least two more. "Okay, put your foot in here, and up you go."

Sundancer didn't move as Kendra found her seat. She looked around wide-eyed. "Wow, this is high."

"Yup. Now take these reins like this." He showed her how to hold them. "Are you ready?"

"Definitely."

He mounted Ace and looked over at her. With her hair down, she made him think of a dark Lady Godiva, but Kendra's hair wasn't that long. It just brushed the top curve of her breasts and her rosy nipples were in full view. He shifted in his saddle, already getting hard. "Okay, let's go."

"What do I do?"

"Nothing. Sundancer will follow Ace." He clicked his tongue and tapped Ace's sides. The well-trained horse started for the canyon and Sundancer followed. He turned around in his saddle to see if Kendra was comfortable and his throat grew tight. Her eyes were glowing with wonder and a smile played at her lips. Her breasts moved with the slow gait of the horse and her naked hips rocked as if she were making love. He snapped his head back to the front and swallowed. He didn't know what he'd done right in his life to deserve her, but he sure as hell would appreciate it.

He led them down the trail he took guests, but halfway around it, he moved off, again looking back to make sure Sundancer followed even though it was an area she hadn't been before. Kendra smiled at him. "This is so beautiful."

"Just wait." He scrutinized his route, not wanting to miss the Joshua tree that would signal the right turn he wanted to make. When he found it, he smiled.

Between the tree and the canyon wall lay an oasis. He moved Ace to the side, clicking his tongue to keep Sundancer coming through the narrow opening.

Kendra's face lit up as she viewed the alcove with its own sandy entryway into a small pool of water. "Oh wow. I didn't know this was here. I can't believe there is still water with how dry it's been."

Wade dismounted and walked over to her. "The creek that runs through your property is fed by the surrounding mountains. It's been raining up there almost every night since I've been here." He lifted his arms up. "Now put your hands on my shoulders and throw your leg over this way."

She did as told and he helped her down. Reluctantly, he let go, but he held on to her hand.

"I didn't know it was raining up there."

He shrugged. "When you've lived here awhile, you'll start to notice those things. Come on, there's more to see."

He carefully led her around the cactus, very aware of her naked skin. As they approached the little pool, the large rock formation became visible.

"Oh Wade, this is amazing."

He stood back and let her explore it just as he did when he'd first found the place while deciding on trails. The rock jutted out in three layers. The bottom one was just above the water in full sun. The second started farther back and provided a large shelf, half of which was covered by the third shelf, which had no overhang at all. What had astounded him was the natural rock steps that made all three levels accessible.

She stood on the second level looking down at him. "This is so unique. Our guests would love it."

Her use of the word "our" made him more confident than ever he'd found the woman of his dreams, though he'd never dreamed of someone so fascinating and perfect for him. "I was thinking more that this could be our special place, when we want to slip away for a few hours. Since we're living at our place of work, this could be a nice retreat."

"I would love that." She carefully made her way down toward him and he met her at the bottom.

"I also thought since we rarely make love in our bed, this might work pretty well for us." Their very different sleep patterns had made daytime sex a must since they were rarely in bed together for very long.

She wrapped her arms around his neck. "I think that's a perfect idea. How about if we christen it now?"

He moved one hand around to grasp her naked ass and cupped the back of her head with his other. "That was my plan." Not giving her a chance to respond, he kissed her hard, his erection in his jeans pressing against her soft mound.

The moan of pleasure in the back of her throat had his balls tightening. Shit, he'd wanted to take it slow, but her need was as strong as his own. With effort, he pulled back. "Help me get off these damn clothes."

She laughed as she pulled down his zipper, releasing him and allowing him to breathe again. "And you were the one who didn't want to go nude."

He paused in unbuttoning his shirt. "Careful, or you'll find yourself in cold water."

She looked over her shoulder. "Hmm, that has possibilities."

He raised a brow at her, but didn't stop undressing. Instead, he whipped off his shirt and threw it on a nearby rock. His hat followed. "Yours too. I want everything exposed."

She didn't hesitate and threw her hat to join his before sitting on a rock to take off her boots.

He sat next to her and did the same then slipped off his jeans. His socks and underwear were next. He helped her to stand. "Are you ready for me?"

She touched her hard nipples. "What do you think?"

Her exhibitionism caused his balls to tense. Impatient, he moved his hand between her legs and stroked the wet juices he found there before pushing two fingers inside.

Her gasp of pleasure fueled his own.

"What about you?" She grasped his cock, tightly stroking up to his wet tip.

He groaned, barely holding back his own orgasm. Shit, his woman was hot. Taking her hand from him, he pulled her to the shallows of the little pool. The coolness of the water gained him some time, but not much.

"Wrap your arms around my neck."

She did, bringing her luscious breasts tight against his chest, her pussy teasing his erection.

"Now wrap your left leg around my waist." When she did, he grasped it, his cock rubbing against her wet folds.

"Now your other one."

"Wade, you're standing. You'll fall."

"Are you challenging my manhood?"

She shook her head. "Never." Grasping him tighter, she lifted her leg up. As she did, he hoisted her with his other arm and tilted his hips, spearing her to his hilt.

"Oh God, Wade." Her shudder vibrated through him, reassuring him she was as close as he was.

Slowly, he stepped back, deeper into the water, its coolness refreshing, but every step moved him back and forth inside her, teasing them. As soon as he'd reached his hips, he stopped, his back firm against the ledge.

"Woman, this one's for you. Love me as you please because afterward I'm going to bend you over this rock and make you come again and then I'm going to take you on top of this rock, spreading your legs wide as I pump into you. Then in the shade on the second rock, I plan to take you against the back wall, and finally, high above us on the top rock, I'm going to tie you down and have you whatever way I want. It's the only way to christen this space properly."

Her moan told him all he needed to know, and he tilted his hips, his cock sliding in deeper.

She immediately took over, her pleasure building his, her body instinctively milking his own. Her hips pumped against him, cool water splashing at his balls. He bent his knees, matching her rhythm, bracing against the rock to give her the most pleasure possible. Then her sheath contracted around him and her body stiffened, sucking at him, pushing him over the edge.

As their mutual shouts filled the hidden alcove, a small hawk took flight. Wade watched it soar as he came down from heights far higher than that. He kissed his love on the forehead and held her tight. Now that he had her, he'd never let her go.

She lifted her head from his shoulder, the rest of her body still holding tight to his. "I think I won that hand. Care to go again?"

Wade laughed. "I'm always ready to go again with you. I told you, cowboys never fold."

~The End~

Unexpected Eden

The Eden Series: Book 2

Coming Spring 2015

For updates, sneak peeks, and special prizes, sign up to receive
the latest news from Lexi at http://eepurl.com/D3MqT

ALSO BY LEXI POST

Masque (http://www.lexipostbooks.com/books/masque/)
Passion's Poison (http://www.lexipostbooks.com/30-2/)
Passion of Sleepy Hollow (http://www.lexipostbooks.com/passion-of-sleepy-hollow/)
Cruise into Eden (The Eden Series: Book 1) (http://www.lexipostbooks.com/cruise-into-eden/)

About Lexi Post

Lexi Post spent years in higher education taking and teaching courses about the classical literature she loved. From Edgar Allan Poe's short story "The Masque of the Red Death" to the 20th century American epic *The Grapes of Wrath*, from *War and Peace* to the *Bhagavad Gita*, she's read, studied, and taught wonderful classics.

But Lexi's first love is romance novels. In an effort to marry her two first loves, she started writing erotic romance inspired by the classics and found she loved it. Her books are known for "erotic romance with a whole lot of story."

Lexi is living her own happily ever after with her husband and her cat Giz. She makes her own ice cream every weekend, loves bright colors, and you will never see her without a hat (unless she is going incognito).

Lexi enjoys hearing from readers. She can be contacted at lexi.post@yahoo.com or through her website www.lexipostbooks.com

For an excerpt from *Cruise into Eden*, Book 1 in The Eden Series, read on.

CRUISE INTO EDEN
BOOK 1 IN THE EDEN SERIES

Chapter One

What had she been thinking to come on a nude cruise?

Erin Danielson maneuvered around the naked people sunning themselves on the deck above the pool, the drone of her mother's voice on her cell phone like white noise in the background of her growing uneasiness. Ascending the stairs to yet another deck, she moved the phone away from her face and sighed in relief as five empty lounge chairs came into view. She brought the phone back. "I'm sure she didn't mean it, Mom. Maybe you took it the wrong way."

Dropping onto the lounge at the end, she tried to keep track of her mother's story, but it was hard to concentrate after all the stares she'd just received. Some people found her sexy new bikini funny, while others looked baffled.

"Erin. Erin. Did you hear that?"

"I'm sorry, Mom. I was distracted for a moment."

"I need you to listen to me. Here I am telling you about the worst insult I've ever had in my life and you— Oh, I have to go, Janice is calling. I'll call you back later."

"But I might not have cell—" The silence on the other end made it clear her mom was long gone. Tucking her phone into her bag, Erin spread her towel and pulled out the coconut 50 SPF suntan lotion. She didn't want to burn on the first full day.

She should never have let Craig talk her into coming on this nude cruise with him. It wasn't as if he was interested in her, not in that way. He had needed her in order to come aboard since it was for couples only, but they were just friends, had been friends for years, like every other man she'd met since she was seventeen. Thank God she'd lost her virginity before then because an eleven-year dry spell had made her desperate enough as it was. Then again, maybe it would have been better if she'd never known what she was missing.

As she covered her legs with lotion, the scent distracted her from her ruminations. She was proud of her legs, but to be fair she had her mom and her running to thank for them. The coconut fragrance had her envisioning warm tropical beaches with aqua-blue waters and maybe a cabana boy. Yes, definitely a hunk of male to fulfill her every need. She shook her head. The chances of that happening were equal to her finding a wormhole on the Lido Deck, and yet she still held out hope.

She couldn't completely blame Craig for her being on the cruise. She'd come aboard for one last attempt. If she couldn't get a man interested in having sex with her on a nude cruise, she would give up the hunt. Besides, this new adventure seemed better than jetting off to Cancun for the eighth time with her friends. She'd lost two of those friends because of her decision to go with Craig. They acted as if they couldn't plan the vacation without her, while they had no problem with Craig backing out.

She smoothed lotion over her flat stomach, shaking her head. Craig, who she'd seen naked in college too many times, was a little too self-involved for her taste. She and her friends were sure the only reason he got drunk was for an excuse to take off his clothes. It didn't surprise her that he wanted to come on a nude cruise.

The least he could have done was come outside with her to rub lotion on her back. He'd never find her two decks above the pool. Last night at dinner, he hadn't stopped scanning the crowd once. Everyone had dressed for the meal, but some of the clothing revealed more than it hid and he had enjoyed the views. This morning he left the cabin butt-naked, and she hadn't seen him since.

She glanced down between the railings at the naked bodies below. The term "clothing optional" cruise was obviously a misnomer. Everyone was naked. Everyone. Old, young, fat, thin, even those with missing parts and scars. She had expected a lot of buff, model-type people, but they weren't. They were like the people she met at home, except they didn't have any clothes on.

It hadn't occurred to her to actually walk around nude. She stood out simply because she chose the "option" of wearing her bright-yellow bikini. She'd never expected to feel uncomfortable because she had her clothes *on*.

She reached over her shoulder as best she could to rub the lotion in. Sighing, she gave up and put it back in her bag and lay down. The motion of the ship was almost nonexistent, but if she concentrated hard, she could feel a slight side-to-side movement as the giant white playground slid through the water. Up this high, the noises from the pool and waterslide were muffled, leaving her in a peaceful haven.

"Excuse me, but are these taken?"

Shading her face with her hand, she opened her eyes to find the most gorgeous man she could imagine, because she was sure she hadn't actually seen a person so perfect. It was as if she'd stepped into a long-lost episode of *Star Trek* and the crew had just discovered heaven. He had to be well over six feet tall. His short, wavy brown hair was a bit messed from the breeze and his dark eyes were set above a perfect, straight nose. His lips curved in a grin that could melt the polar ice cap, and was definitely causing her own temperature to rise. The dark stubble along his chin gave him a rugged look that said he had a bit more testosterone than she was usually treated to. He appeared to have a round tattoo of some kind on his left biceps, but she couldn't tell what it was from where she sat. She let her gaze move lower to find large pectoral muscles with no sign of hair followed by a six-pack a bodybuilder would kill for.

She couldn't help but look lower only to flush at the sight of a very large cock nestled above a significant ball sac. Snapping her gaze back to his face, she shook her head. "Hmm, uh, no, they aren't taken."

"Do you mind if we join you?" His deep, slightly accented voice brought her senses into hyperalert and it took her a moment to understand what he'd said.

"We?"

"Yes, my friend and me." He pointed to her right and she forced herself to stop looking at him only to find another feast for her eyes.

She had to be dreaming. Maybe she was in some kind of time warp and had been whisked away to another planet because there was no way men like this existed on Earth. The second man had long black hair and eyes that seemed lighter than the other's, but she couldn't tell the color because the sun was behind him. His cheekbones were high and his chin sharper than his companion's. His lips, however, were distinctively full, which had her licking her own. Luckily, he didn't smile and simply nodded once.

The sun suddenly became stifling, so she sat up. "Of course you can join me." She stared as the long-haired man walked around the other one, lifted a lounge chair with his free hand and bent over to set it on the other side of her, giving her a view of the back of his taut thigh muscles, ass, and balls. Holy shit. She might come just looking at these two.

Wait. If these two men were together, they must be a couple. Her blood cooled. Damn, just her luck.

"My name is Nassic Wild, but everyone calls me Nase." The first man held out his hand.

She grasped it silently, still reeling from the man's attractiveness and his unobtainability.

Nase grinned. "My friend is Wareson Night, but we call him Ware."

She looked at the other man, who once again simply nodded. "Ware? Like in Werewolf?"

Nase laughed. "There's no such thing as a werewolf."

She attempted a smile, still too blown away by their physicality to be sure she succeeded.

"And you are?"

Nase's voice sent her senses into hyper mode. "Oh, I'm sorry. I'm Erin Danielson."

The man's gaze shifted to Ware for a moment before he looked at her again. "It's nice to *meet* you, Erin."

Now what was that about? He said the word "meet" as if he'd heard of her, but that couldn't be. Unless Craig had sent them up to show her what she couldn't have. If he'd done that, she would kick him out of their stateroom so fast he'd skin his bare ass on the doorsill on his way out.

Nase stepped in front of her, blocking the sun for a moment, helping her body to cool a bit. "I'm going to the bar to grab a couple beers. Would you like anything?"

"I would love a bottled water."

"A bucket of beers and a couple waters on the way." Nase strode off, completely comfortable in his nudity, and Erin completely comfortable with the view of his rounded backside.

She glanced at Ware, who now sat on the lounge chair next to her rubbing lotion on his bulging biceps. Above those massive muscles on his right shoulder was what looked like natural beauty marks, but they were in an odd shape, two dots in a row above three dots in a row. Despite the fact the man was as dark as someone from Greece, they stood out clearly. How odd.

She stared as Ware protected his skin, *all* of his skin. The man had no tan lines. He was a bit bigger than Nase, and broader, but not by much. He still hadn't said anything, and she suddenly wanted to hear his voice. "Have you taken a nude cruise before?"

He stilled mid-rub and looked at her. His gaze was intense and now that he was next to her, she could see his eyes were a forest green. Absolutely breathtaking, though it could have been her anticipation of his voice that had her holding her breath.

"No. This is our first one."

The deepness of his tone wrapped around her like a cocoon that she never wanted to leave. His accent was heavier, but from where? The tension she felt around Nase disappeared with Ware, which left her clearheaded enough to remember the two men were a couple and she had no right to ogle them. "This is my first one, too. Though I'm not sure I will ever get into the 'nude' part." She forced herself to stop staring at Ware's perfect male body. She closed her eyes and lay back on her lounge.

"Why?"

The dark, sensuous voice slid over her skin again, and she could feel him looking at her. No, not looking, exploring her with his sight. She opened her eyes and watched him. Every place he viewed suddenly became sensitized, as if he had lightly run his fingers along her body. She swore she could feel his gaze as it traveled across her stomach, up her ribs, over her breasts, along her neck, and through her hair until she found his eyes riveted on hers. "Why?"

"Yes. Why would you not allow your body to enjoy the sun fully?"

She pushed her hair behind her ear. "I… I—It's hard to explain."

He cocked his head and stared intently at her.

Obviously her answer had not satisfied him. "I'm guessing you are not American. In my country, we wear clothes all the time. It's what we're used to. I know there are a few countries that are more open about nakedness, but I'm not from those."

"I believe many of the people on this ship are from America."

Erin was too focused on the extra emphasis he left on the final letter "a" in "America" to at first grasp his point. When she did, she flushed. "True, but I never knew they existed. This is all very new to me. I just learned last night why there are piles of towels in the main areas of the boat. I guess everyone is supposed to use them to sit on if they are nude. I'm sure I'll learn a lot more about this by the end of the week."

As if her answer had pleased him, he went back to rubbing lotion on his dark body. She couldn't help but watch as he finished covering his hard stomach, but as his hand dipped between his legs, she closed her eyes tight. The last thing she needed was to have an orgasm watching a gay man put on suntan lotion. Luckily, Craig had stayed out late last night, so she'd been able to pleasure herself. Maybe she should be a bit more appreciative of her roommate's habits.

She sensed Nase's return and opened her eyes. Shielding her face, she swallowed hard. The man moved with confidence. It was as if the air parted before him. If she were air, she would stand in his way and let him push that large cock, that swayed as he walked, right up against her. His thigh muscles rippled as he strode and too soon he had dropped onto the lounge next to her.

"Here you are. One bottled water for now and another in the bucket for later." He held out the water. She sat up and shook off the condensation before opening it. Taking a gulp, the cold liquid glided down her throat, cooling her a bit until it hit her stomach.

"Ware." Nase lobbed an open bottle of Heineken over her to his friend who caught it effortlessly, not a drop spilled. These two had obviously been together a long time. She wanted to know more, but it would be a waste of time. The cruise rules were everyone had to be with someone. The organizers did not want people coming on the cruise to try to hook-up. That's why Craig had needed her, so he could pretend he was part of a couple. She'd like to think the men flanking her had done the same thing, but she doubted it. They were too familiar with each other.

Nase opened another beer, a foreign brand she didn't recognize and took a few swallows. The cords in his neck moved as he chugged the liquid. His tanned skin glistened with sweat and she licked her lips to keep herself from licking him. When he brought the bottle down, he faced her, his legs spread wide, his cock on display.

Sunglasses. Why had she left her sunglasses in the room? She just wouldn't look. It would be impolite.

"So what is your life like?" Nase leaned his elbows on his knees, distracting her from his question for a moment. His tight forearms sprinkled with dark hair had her body revving.

A low noise from her other side returned her attention to the topic. "My life? Do you mean what I do for a living?"

Nase shrugged, and took another sip of beer.

"I'm an IT manager for a science fiction television station that sells stuff online. Actually, it's more like a district manager as my boss has many product centers under his purview and I'm his right-hand man. It's a good job that I can leave at the office. What about you?"

Nase grinned. "I'm in defense, but I can't talk about it." He gestured toward Ware with his beer. "He's in government. Very into laws and justice and what's fair."

Erin turned to find Ware on his back watching her. She took another sip of water. "So I guess you do take your work home."

"Always," Nase grumbled. "That man is always thinking. He needs to have more fun. Maybe on this cruise."

She nodded halfheartedly. Yup, they were definitely a couple. It was too heartbreaking to contemplate any further. Taking another sip of water, she capped her bottle and lay back on the lounge chair.

"Why do you wear clothes?"

She opened one eye and looked at Nase. She wanted to be irritated, but he was just too attractive to be mad at. "I'm exercising the option to be clothed."

At her answer, his brows lowered. "But you're gorgeous. Stunning. And you have a sexy body. I would think you would be proud to show it."

She flushed from the inside out at his words.

"And I bet your breasts are perfectly round with strong, hard nipples that beg to be sucked."

Even as moisture gathered between her legs, Ware interrupted. "Nase." The single word said low and sternly was enough. The other man shook his head in puzzlement and settled in to apply lotion to his own taut body.

Erin closed her eyes tightly and tried to relax. How could she let a gay man make her wet? She must be more desperate than she realized. But to be fair, the men on either side of her were sinfully built and no one could blame her.

Wait. Why were they on either side of her? If they were a couple, wouldn't they want to be next to each other? Then again, they could simply be protecting her. She had a couple gay friends who would do that, kind of look out for her. That must be it. Still, she could certainly dream if she wanted to, and she would, next time she had the chance to relieve her fast-growing sexual need.